THE

AMBER TRAIL

M. J. KELLY

1

THE HARDEST MOMENTS IN A PERSON'S life don't come with a warning. They don't give you time to prepare, to psyche yourself up, to make sure you get enough sleep the night before. They sneak up unannounced and give you a cold, hard slap in the face that can change your outlook on life in an instant.

Dig Buckley certainly went into the hardest moment of his life unprepared. In fact, with it rapidly approaching, he was already breathing hard and cultivating wide crescents of sweat under his armpits as he worked at shifting forty cases of beer into the back of a boxy white truck.

The morning was hot, the type that punished any attempt at physical exercise. Dig crossed a white gravel driveway between two buildings, an aged suburban house of red-brick on one side, and a tall warehouse of new aluminium on the other. Its shiny panelling reflected the sunlight directly into Dig's eyes.

Inside the warehouse, he squatted beside a pallet stacked knee high with pale orange cases of beer. He gripped two cases and lifted, then trudged them slowly across the drive as gravel crunched under his feet.

"Hey, Dig."

Dig paused momentarily, then continued on. When he reached the truck, he slung the cases into the back tray with a thud.

"Hey Dimwit, you listening?"

Dig turned to face his older brother Jake.

"You have to go help Dad." Jake's eyes were bloodshot, and his dress shirt creased.

Dig pushed past his brother and hoisted two more cases of beer to his chest. "I thought you were helping him today."

"Nope. Important sales meeting at the casino. Wilson himself called me up...says he's thinking of serving our beer. I'm meeting him for lunch today."

"Can't you see I'm busy at the moment? In fact, would you mind helping me load a few of these?"

"Why don't you use the forklift?"

"It broke down."

Jake glanced at the pallet and shrugged. "Already told you bro. Important meeting. Someone's got to find customers for all this stock. Can't keep Wilson waiting." He leaned inside the truck and ripped the cardboard away from one of the cases.

"Hey! Leave it."

Jake lifted two six-packs, one in each hand. "Better take some samples too. Important contract this one."

"Screw you."

"No thanks." Jake walked up the driveway toward a bank of cars near the road. "I'm taking the work car," he shouted as the park lights flashed on a blue sedan. "And don't forget Dad. He's waiting for you out back."

Dig shook his head. He reached into the truck to retrieve the half-empty case, and moved it to a shelf inside the building. Footsteps then returned from the drive.

"Need to find my...sales folder," Jake said.

"It's in the boot."

"My folder?"

"No, your squash racquet. I saw it there last night."

Jake opened his mouth, then closed it again. He gave a sarcastic smile and dropped his head as he trudged stiffly back up the driveway.

"And also," Dig shouted. "Wilson was on the news this morning, on a boat in Portugal. So I don't reckon he's turning up to your important meeting."

Jake raised his arm through the car window, his middle finger extended. The engine roared to life and the car reversed out to the road.

Dig watched him leave, then wiped the sweat from his forehead with the shoulder of his T-shirt. He turned and walked down to the rear of the red brick house via a patch of faded grass, flapping the base of his shirt with two hands, trying to work up some breeze on his sweaty midriff.

Behind the house, the grass stretched out to create a modest backyard. A rusted Hills Hoist washing line stood lopsided in one corner. A barbeque sat in the other, covered in cobwebs. On the far edge of the grass, a rocky drop fell to a forest of gum trees and wirey shrubs, marking the edge of the property and the start of public bushland.

His father stood on the grass, positioning a ladder against the gutter of the house. He wore a faded pair of blue football shorts. A pale singlet tan was etched around the grey hairs on his chest and a tool belt hung from his waist.

"You going to help me, or come up with a fake excuse like your brother?"

"Depends if I can think one up in time," Dig said, smiling. "Might cost you though."

"Really? Well that's fine. You can take it out of the rent this week...oh hang on, you don't actually *pay* rent." He raised an eyebrow. "In that case, I'll give you some imaginary money, and you can give it back to me as imaginary rent."

Dig laughed. Since his twenty-first birthday, the hints from his parents that it was time to move out were becoming increasingly less subtle. "Okay, maybe this one's on the house."

"It'll be on the house all right." His father passed him a pair of gloves. "The ladder's already set up."

They spent the morning replacing roof tiles, and as they slotted the final piece into place, Dig's father nodded and surveyed their work. "There. No more water drippin' on my head while I watch the footy."

"How are my hard working boys going?" Dig's mother shouted from below. She stood in the front drive, wearing a floral dress; her hair was up in a bun. "You want something to drink?"

"Nah. We'll grab something when we get down."

"He working you hard Dig?"

"Slave driver."

She smiled and held a hand up to shield the sun. "I'm going to pick up something for lunch."

"Great."

His mother fumbled through her purse to find her car keys, and waved again as she backed out the drive.

Dig sat on the crest of the roof to catch his breath. A light breeze blew through his hair and a lawnmower whirred from a neighbour's yard. From this vantage point, they had a 360 degree view. Beside them was the imposing shape of the new warehouse, freshly built on the other side of the drive. A sign hung from the building, facing the street.

BUCKLEY'S BREWERY

Home of Australia's Favourite Pale Ale

BUCKLEY'S CHANCE

"Looks good, huh?" Dig said. "The new building."

"Yep."

"You ever think you'd build your own brewery next door?"

"Nope, happened pretty quickly."

They gazed out over the treeline to the expanse of bush beyond. The cicadas had started up in a buzzing wall of noise.

"Man I love the view up here," his dad said, smiling. Crow's feet bunched in the corners of his brown eyes; his mess of dark hair waved in the breeze.

Dig nodded. "It's awesome."

"You know, sometimes I think about building a platform up here and sticking a couple of beanbags on it in the evenings. We could watch the sun go down with some of the stock."

"I like it."

His father pointed to a small clearing in the trees. A glint of water shimmered behind the branches. "Waterhole's looking good."

Dig lifted his head, straining for a better look. "Perfect day for a swim."

"Wanna head down there?"

"Now?"

His father shrugged. "Just a quick dip before lunch."

"Sure."

They descended from the roof and headed inside. Dig changed his clothes and walked out to the back deck, where his father was waiting in swimmers, holding two bottles of beer. The labels read *Buckley's Chance*. "Quality control," he said, grinning.

They followed a winding dirt track down into the bush until it reached the edge of the creek, where it turned right and ran parallel to the sandy bank. After fifteen minutes the path turned the last corner to reveal their destination.

The waterhole was a clear expanse, around the size of a tennis court, and framed by pale, knobbly gum trees with bark peeling from their trunks. The creek cascaded into the pool, sending ripples across the surface that reflected the sunlight, inviting them to jump in. Hidden frogs called out from the reeds.

Dig's father stepped down to a flat section of rock on the water's edge and placed the two beers beside the pool. "Yee ha!" He launched himself at the water, executing a haphazard bomb that sent a plume of liquid into the air.

Dig was close behind him, diving in; the cool water bit refreshingly at his skin. He returned to the surface with the familiar earthy taste of the creek water on his lips. It reminded him of his childhood.

"Great day huh?" His father was treading water with wet hair stuck flat on the side of his head.

"Awesome."

His father swam a few strokes and lifted himself to sit on the rock platform at the edge of the pool, his legs dangling. Dig followed, and sat beside him. The trickling of the waterfall filled the air.

"Would sir care for some refreshment?" His father held out one of the bottles.

"Certainly, my good man."

They clinked the necks together before taking a couple of long drafts.

"You kids were always good swimmers."

Dig held up his left foot. Two of the middle toes were webbed together with skin—a minor condition that he had lived with since birth. "Well it's easier to swim when we inherit deformities like this."

His father held up his own foot, where the same two toes were webbed together. "Deformity's the wrong word...I call it a genetic advancement."

Dig shook his head and took another mouthful. Silhouettes of the trees reflected on the water surface.

His father abruptly lurched his head forward, gagging the contents of his mouth onto the rock between his legs. The bottle slipped from his grasp and shattered on the platform with a pop, scattering glass fragments into the water.

Dig stared at his father. "You okay?"

His father didn't answer. His head was bowed forward between his thighs and his mouth was open; saliva dripped from his lips. He gagged again, and coughed, and a small object fell from his mouth to the ground, where it sat waterlogged—twisting and flapping in the creases of the rock.

Dig looked closer. It was an insect, with a thick orange body covered in hairy black stripes. A pointed black stinger throbbed from its rear.

It was a wasp.

"Dad?"

"Bugger." His father pulled himself roughly to his feet, clutching at his neck. "Must have flown into my beer."

"Did it sting you?"

He nodded. "Got me in the throat."

"Aren't you—"

"Allergic? Yep." He swallowed, wincing with pain.

"Don't you have some kind of antidote needle?"

"The Epipen? Left it back at the house."

Dig pursed his lips.

"Well I haven't been stung since I was a kid." His father frowned. "And I didn't think we'd be down here long."

"But if your throat starts swelling up..."

His father nodded.

"We need to get you to a doctor."

Dig's first instinct was to grab for a mobile phone, but they didn't bring one. They only had their swimmers and sandals with them, and a half empty beer.

"Let's go," Dig said.

They pulled on their shoes and turned for home. They had about two kilometres to travel, but suddenly that seemed like a marathon distance.

Dig let his dad take the lead, settling in behind him as he broke into the stiff jog of a man whose knees had given up running years before. Dig jogged a few paces behind, trying to let his dad set a pace he was comfortable with—but adrenaline was pumping in his veins, and he had to restrain himself from running the track at a sprinter's pace.

The first section of the track climbed up and over a large rocky outcropping. They stepped from rock to rock in big strides, trying to maintain balance in their sandals.

The track levelled out as they passed through the rocks, and trees gathered close to the track, pitching eucalyptus branches out over their heads. The sun splintered through the leaves, throwing shadows at their feet.

Dig's breathing increased, and he tried to keep an eye on his father—who was jogging with his head tilted forward and his mouth open. His cheeks were pink and dots of sweat lined his forehead. Dig could hear his breathing, and he noticed it had taken on a rasping quality, his chest heaving in and out in time with his steps. Dig tried to ignore it, but he knew what it was. It was the sound of an airway closing in on itself.

"How're you doing?"

His father glanced back and smiled weakly. "I'm...okay," he said. "We'll get there". He continued in a stiff jog, his shoulders hunched, his eyes staring forward.

A tree branch hung over the track ahead of them; it caught his father's face and flung back in Dig's direction. Dig dodged away and regained his stride. The next time he looked up, he saw the branch had sliced a red strip across his father's cheek, just below his eye. A bead of blood tracked down his face, but his father didn't seem to notice.

Dig tried to remain calm. The adrenaline rush he'd ridden to this point was bottoming out, and replaced by fatigue. Sweat poured from his body, running down his chest and face; his head felt like a furnace. He was sure his father must be feeling much worse.

They followed the track for a few minutes as it wound down through a swampy section of high grass. The ground was mushy here, and his father's strides shortened to a shuffle. His arms hung low at his sides and his face was red; the tip of his tongue hung on his lower lip like a slug.

The track snaked out of the swamp and up a small rise, and his father dropped the pace back down to a walk. His hands went to his head, and for the first time Dig noticed swelling on his face and neck. His left eye was puffy, and partially closed.

His dad tilted back his head and took in three deep breaths—a sound like air being sucked through a wet straw. His torso swayed left, and with a dull thud his foot caught hard on a tree root protruding from the track. He pitched forward and reached out, but took the impact on his shoulder. He rolled to his back, eyes closed, gasping and wincing with pain. Brown sand clung to his arm and chest.

Dig fell beside him. "Dad!"

His father opened his eyes briefly, then closed them again. His bare chest rose and fell rapidly as he took in shallow, ragged breaths. "Just...need...to get...my breath back."

Panic churned in Dig's stomach. *This can't be happening,* he thought.

His father's breathing regulated slightly, and he lifted his head and opened his eyes.

"Dad." Dig's eyes were wide. "I'm going to run ahead and bring the needle back."

His dad reached out with a clammy hand to grab Dig's forearm. His forehead was creased in fear. "No," he said. "Just stay with me. I can get there."

Dig clenched his teeth, nodded slowly, and grabbed his father below the armpit to hoist him to his feet. They stood together on the track for a moment, shoulder to shoulder, covered in dirt and sweat.

After a few deep breaths, his father took a step forward and they moved away in a brisk walk. Dig kept his arm hooked around his side, supporting him the best he could.

How far had they run? Dig thought. *Halfway? More than that?* His concept of time was skewed. He tried to gauge his position on the track.

They trudged along, step by step, following the trail as it snaked through the shadows of trees by the creek. Up this close, Dig couldn't ignore his father's laboured breathing, which had slowly developed into a wet bubbling in the back of his throat.

Finally, the track broke away from the creek and turned up to the house. They were almost home.

As they walked up the first rock step, his father coughed and retched out a sticky glob of phlegm that fell forward and hung from the end his chin, wobbling in time with his step. Dig wiped it away with the back of his hand. His father's face was bloated, and his left eye swollen shut.

"Come on Dad! Nearly there!" he said, but Dig could feel the energy depleting from his father's body. His steps were slower and his balance off, until Dig felt like he was supporting his whole weight, willing him to take one pace after the other.

"Come on Dad!" Tears ran down Dig's face. "Help!" he shouted towards the house, the waterhole, the sky. "Help us, please!" The words echoed around the bush and returned to him.

His father took two more shuffling steps, and then tipped forward. Dig tried to support him, but his body slipped from his sweat soaked grasp. He landed heavily on his back against the trunk of a gum tree.

His father opened his good eye and looked upward. "I'm sorry...bud." His face had a blue tinge, and his breathing was a shallow wheeze. "Can't...do it." He grabbed Dig's arm and met his eyes. "Listen," he said in a weak, croaky voice. "The brewery...is not...what you think. If I go...you should...shut it down."

"Forget work!" Dig stood over him. "Where do you keep the needle?"

"Tell Max...the deal...is off...no more...packages."

"Shut up!" Dig screamed. "*Where's the bloody needle?*"

"My...sock drawer."

"Okay. I'll be back." His father nodded.

Dig sprinted up the remaining track at a breakneck pace, ducking and weaving through foliage at the side of path that ripped at his torso. When he reached the house, he bounded up the steps at the side of the building, through the back door and into the kitchen.

His mother stood at the kitchen counter, unpacking groceries. The radio played Frank Sinatra. She looked up, and her expression dropped.

"Dad's in trouble," Dig said, breathing hard. "We need to call an ambulance."

She looked at him blankly. "What?"

"He was stung by a wasp...and is having trouble breathing."

"He's allergic!" she said in a high pitch.

"I know!" Dig ran past her into the hallway. "We need to find his Epipen!" At the end of the hall he turned into his parent's bedroom.

His mother's voice echoed down the corridor behind him. "—in his sock drawer."

Dig skirted around the neatly-made bed and yanked open the top drawer of the dresser. The drawer pulled out completely and the contents fell to the floor.

He crouched and scrambled amongst the paired socks and underwear until he found what he was looking for—a thin, pen shaped object that had *Epinephrine Auto-Injector* written on the side. He grabbed it and scrambled back out of the room, striking his shin on the corner of the bed.

He passed his mother in the hall. She held her phone to her ear. Her eyebrows were drawn together. "Where is he?"

"Down the bush track, not far..." Dig bounded through the kitchen, out the back door and across the deck. His mother followed behind him, speaking to emergency services as she jogged.

His father lay on his back beneath the large gum, his face turned up to the sky. Dig was relieved to see that his chest was moving shallowly. He knelt beside him and fumbled with the needle.

"Oh Shaun!" his mother whimpered as she knelt on the other side. She held a bottle of water in a trembling hand, and lowered it to his mouth. The liquid bubbled between his lips, only to dribble away and run down his cheek.

Dig grabbed his father's leg and positioned the Epipen over his thigh, then jammed down the catch, firing the needle into the muscle.

His father's good eye opened and darted around. He met his wife's gaze, and his breath laboured in his throat with a sickening constricted squeal; the words came out slow and punctuated. "I'm...sorry...guys."

"Shaun!" His mother grasped his hand, her fingernails digging into the skin. "Come on now, breathe!" A curtain of her hair fell from its bun and hung over her face. Tears ran down her cheeks.

The wail of an ambulance approached in the distance, before filling the air, then shutting down altogether.

Dig ran the short distance up the track to see the ambulance screech to a stop outside the house. Two paramedics, a petite blonde woman and a big bald guy, leapt out of the vehicle, equipment in hand.

"This way!" Dig shouted. "Quick!" He led them down the track.

His mother was hunched over her husband when they arrived, cradling his head, panicked. "He's stopped breathing!" The paramedics took over, starting CPR, and injecting further drugs into his arm.

Dig pulled his mother gently to her feet and led her a distance up the track. The CPR wasn't something they needed to see. She fell to her rear, clutching the bottle of water to her forehead like a crucifix. "Oh please," she whispered. "Please God."

Dig sat beside her with an arm on her shoulder. Tears ran down his face, uncontrolled.

Above him, the cicadas sang uninterrupted in the trees. A bird with feathers of green and blue crossed the sky.

Eventually, the female paramedic approached them. "Mrs. Buckley?"

Dig's mother looked up. Her eyes were red and wet.

"We're sorry. But your husband isn't responding to treatment. He had a severe allergic reaction, and there wasn't enough time for the Epinephrine to arrest it."

The energy drained from Dig's body and he closed his eyes. *This can't be real,* he thought.

But unfortunately it was. And even worse, it was just the start of the upheaval to come.

2

DIG SAT WITH SLUMPED SHOULDERS in the lounge room of the family home as an overhead fan pushed warm air down from the ceiling. His mother sat beside him, holding a handkerchief; her hair hung over her face in ragged strands. Dig's grandfather paced on the opposite side of the room, his furry eyebrows knitted together as he mouthed words to himself.

A straight-backed policewoman wrote into a small notebook. Dig's mother spoke to the woman between long pauses, during which she would squint and hold her handkerchief up to her mouth.

An engine whined outside the house, followed by a screech of rubber on asphalt. The screen door thumped open and Jake stood in the doorway, wearing shorts and a damp sports shirt. His cheeks were pink, and he stared wildly around the room.

"How the hell...?"

His mother opened her mouth to speak, then pressed her lips together as her face contorted into a new grimace.

Dig's grandfather stepped toward Jake, holding out an open arm. "It was an accident."

Jake's eyebrows drew together. "That's a fucking understatement."

"An allergic reaction. Came out of nowhere."

"Yeah right." Jake glanced at Dig, then crouched beside his mother.

Dig's head fell back to the couch, and his eyes fixed on a framed photo hanging skew on the opposite wall. It was a family shot, taken four years previously at his cousin's wedding. In the photo, Dig's parents stood with their two sons, arms around each other, catching a rare moment of family harmony. It was a moment that was gone, and could never be repeated.

Over the next week, friends and relatives arrived at the house with pitying looks on their faces, and presented the family with flowers and dishes of rubbery lasagne. Dig moved about the house like a zombie, nodding yes to most of the questions put to him as the preparations for the funeral began.

The nominated day arrived on a cloudy Tuesday morning. Dig found a barely-worn suit at the back of his cupboard, put it on, and walked out to the front driveway where his mother stood by the car. Jake sat in the driver's seat, gazing vacantly ahead.

As Dig reached the vehicle a rapping sound echoed from across the driveway, and he turned to see a thin-faced man standing at the door to the brewery office. Two broad-shouldered men loitered further up the drive. The three men seemed to be of Indian descent, wearing dark suits and ties. The thin-faced man continued to knock loudly on the door.

Dig crossed the driveway. "Can I help you?"

The man took a step forward and smiled, revealing dark, deep-set eyes. His colleagues approached behind him—they looked like thugs that had just stepped away from the door of a nightclub.

"Hello," the man said in an Indian accent. "We're looking for Shaun Buckley. We have a meeting with him today."

Dig glanced back toward his family and took a deep breath. "I'm sorry guys, but I've got some bad news. Shaun died this week in an accident."

The man's smile dropped from his face. "He...has died?"

"Yes." Dig scratched at his ear. "It was pretty sudden. We tried to let everyone know but...obviously we must've missed a few."

"Oh." The men exchanged glances. "We're sorry to hear that."

"Yeah. It's been a tough week."

They stood in silence for a moment.

"Dig!" his brother shouted. "What's happening?"

"You go! I'll take the other car."

Jake frowned before backing the car out of the drive.

"I hope you don't mind me asking," the man said. "But is anyone handling your father's business affairs now?"

"We hope to get things moving again next week. But at this stage the brewery's shut down."

The men glanced at each other again, then nodded. "Thank you."

"No prob." Dig took a few steps toward the car, then turned back. "Hey, if you want to go, the funeral's on today...it's at ten at St Mary's church up the road."

"Yes, we may attend. Your father was a good man."

"Thanks. You're all welcome."

The man tipped his head in a small bow, then led his companions up the driveway to the street.

The small church swelled with people during the service. Light streamed through stained glass windows, and the smell of burning incense competed with the perfume of the pale blue flowers piled before the altar. His mother stood frail in a black dress.

The service was long, and Dig found it hard to concentrate. His father's coffin, a glossy brown box with solid silver handles, was propped up front and centre in the church. Dig watched the coffin for a long time, his mind drifting, remembering the last time he had seen his father alive—sprawled on his back, struggling to breathe. Scared. Dying.

That's the hardest part about death, he thought. *Most of the time people go out of this life feeling scared or in pain—or most likely both. And there's little we can do to avoid it.*

At the conclusion of the service, they walked the coffin up the aisle and outside to the waiting hearse. The family stood with the congregation as the vehicle pulled into the street, heading for the crematorium. Everyone stood silent for a moment, then Dig's grandfather cleared his throat.

"The family would like to thank everyone for coming," he said from the top of the steps outside the church. "And we now invite everyone back to the house to have a drink in Shaun's memory."

Dig drove back to the house with his mother. They were first to arrive home, and as they reached the front door Dig noticed that it was hanging ajar. He stopped and frowned.

He exchanged a look with his mother, then gave the door a push. It caught against something heavy on the opposite side. Dig surveyed the drive behind him, then turned and pushed the door again, harder, forcing enough space between the door and jamb for him to squeeze into the front passage.

Inside the house, a black ceramic umbrella stand lay flat across the beige carpet, wedged behind the door. A mess of umbrellas were spread beside it, along with a chunk of jagged timber that contained the housing for the door lock. Dig looked back to the jamb and saw it had been smashed clean away from the frame.

Dig whispered to his mother. "Someone broke in." She stiffened and dug through her purse for a phone.

Dig stepped further into the house. Beams of sunlight fell diagonally through the hallway windows, illuminating dancing clouds of dust. He tilted his head. A low hum and muffled clanking could be heard from inside.

He knelt and picked up a long umbrella with a solid wooden handle, and brandished it loosely behind him like a baseball bat, his stomach knotting as he tiptoed across the passage toward the kitchen doorway. When he reached the opening he swallowed, then moved through quickly—arms up, ready to strike.

The room was a mess. Cupboards lay open with their contents spewed on the floor. Cushions from the couch were piled against the wall. The fridge freezer door was ajar, and water dripped from it to form a wide, wet puddle on the tiles. But the room was otherwise empty; Dig allowed himself to breathe.

The noise remained, and louder now, a clattering rumble combined with a tinkling of shattered glass. It was the sound of breakage and destruction, and it was coming from the back of the house, toward the bedrooms. Dig's grip on the umbrella tightened until his knuckles turned white.

He stepped through the kitchen with his stomach churning. As he reached the counter he spotted a timber block brimming with knife handles. He placed the umbrella carefully on the bench, and selected the largest knife of the collection—with a ceramic handle, wide steel blade and pointed tip. He held it up with a shaking hand, took another breath, and stepped into the hallway that led to the back of the house.

As he entered the passage, Dig stopped and listened. The crashing, crunching sound echoed from the far end of the hall, behind the closed laundry door. His hands were clammy, and he wiped them on his shirt before he tiptoed forward.

As he passed the open doors of the three bedrooms he saw further evidence of destruction: wardrobes thrown open; boxes of shoes tipped out on bedspreads; side drawers emptied onto the carpet; and mattresses pulled up and dumped against the wall.

He reached the end of the hallway and stood before the laundry door, where the noise was loud and immediate. Dig clenched his teeth, then twisted the handle and flung the door open. He stepped into the room, eyes wide.

A heavy, humid heat billowed into his face. The room was covered in white tile, and a washing machine, dryer and sink lined up along one wall. Natural light streamed through a glass door on the opposite side, leading to the backyard. Dig scanned the room—ready to shout, ready to fight, ready to run.

But nobody was there. The room was empty. He exhaled.

Above his head, square timber cupboards lay open; at his feet, bottles of bleach lay strewn across the tile. Though the room was empty, the sound remained—a loud clunking and tinkling through a resonant hum. He glanced down and saw the dryer was rumbling by his knees. It was a front loading model, and through the glass viewer something churned in the vortex of the internal tumbler.

Dig looked back down the empty hallway, blinking rapidly, then squatted in front of the dryer. He examined the buttons on the machine and pressed the catch on the door. It popped open and the power cut out, and the contents settled to the bottom of the tumbler drum with a final clatter and crash of glass. Smoke billowed from the opening with a stench of burnt paper and ammonia.

Dig prodded the door further open with one finger, and leaned in for a closer inspection. Stuck in the lower corners of the tumbler baffles were piles of splintered black timber and broken glass. Dig squinted closer and saw that nestled amongst the shards was a darkened rectangle of paper. He reached inside and gingerly lifted it out by one corner. The paper was thick and warm, and sticky to touch, and after he extracted the curled rectangle from the machine he balanced it in the centre of his palm.

Its edges were dark and burnt, but the shadowy silhouettes of four people could be made out on the square. Dig recognised it as a family photograph—the same family photograph that up until this morning had resided in the middle of the lounge room wall.

Dig stared at the picture, then glanced at the shards of timber and glass in the dryer. A shiver of unease rippled through his spine.

"Dig? Are you here?" It was his brother's voice.

"In the laundry."

Jake stood in the doorway and his eyes darted around the room. His mother appeared behind him.

"What kind of sick bastard breaks into a house while people are at a funeral?" Jake said.

"A smart one," Dig said. "You can be sure that nobody's home." He passed the photo to Jake.

Jake frowned. "Is that from the lounge?"

Dig nodded. "I found it cooking in the clothes dryer. The whole thing was in there, frame and all, smashed to bits."

Jake swore under his breath and shook his head. "If I ever catch who did this, I'm going to rip their head off."

Outside, the wail of a police siren approached from the distance. His mother took the photo from Jake and studied it. "We need to forget this for now," she said. "I'll deal with the police. You guys help the people arriving for the wake. We can send everyone out to the back deck." She looked them both in the eye. "And no jealous fighting between you boys today either."

The brothers glanced at each other, then nodded.

3

AS PEOPLE ARRIVED FOR THE WAKE, they presented Dig with cards and flowers. The back deck filled shoulder-to-shoulder, and the hum of conversation filled the air. His mother had prepared tables of wilting sandwiches and cubed cheese. Tubs of *Buckley's Chance* lay in beds of ice at their feet.

Jake stood at the railing with two of Dig's older cousins—solid, rugby-playing guys with crewcuts and broad shoulders. They rationed out large helpings from a bottle of whisky.

Dig did his best to socialise. "It was a beautiful service," said his grey-haired neighbour as he fiddled with the label of his beer.

"Yes, very moving," said the neighbour's wife beside him.

Dig nodded and tried to muster a smile, but his mind was elsewhere. He couldn't stop thinking about the break-in. The house had been full of people that morning—dressing for the funeral and preparing for the wake—then as they stood in the church, a stranger had ransacked through their personal belongings with no regard for sentiment or pity.

"Everyone." Dig's grandfather startled him from his thoughts. He stood at the head of the deck, his face etched with wrinkles. "I'd like to say a few words." The conversation dropped to a murmur.

"First, thanks everyone for coming. It means a lot to see you here. The last week has been difficult to say the least, and the family thanks you for your support." He pursed his lips. "For Shaun to be taken from us in such a sudden and tragic way is...an unthinkable heartbreak." He blinked rapidly and dropped his head before continuing.

"Shaun was a great man. Fiercely loyal to his family, a great father, a trusted friend, and a man who had the courage to follow his passions." He lifted a bottle of beer from a tub beside his feet. "Shaun started his life as a pretty average bricklayer, but during that time the back shed was always full of sacks of malt and hops, and he'd work the mash tun long into the night." Dig's neighbour smiled and nodded.

"He made a few average beers in the early years, and quite a lot of bad ones. It wasn't until he spent some time researching the craft on travels through Europe and Asia that he developed the knowledge, and found the right *ingredients*, to create a beer that wasn't just good, but absolutely world class. The new brewery that you see behind you is testament to his skill and hard work. Buckley's Chance is fast becoming Australia's most applauded and awarded craft beer, and will soon be sold in every state. I hope every time we drink a Buckley's Chance in the years to come, we stop and remember who Shaun was, and what he left behind." He turned to Dig's mother and smiled weakly. She raised her bottle up at him with her lips pressed thin.

"If everyone could please lift their drinks, I'd like to raise a toast." He held his bottle up. "To Shaun," he said. "We'll miss him like hell."

"To Shaun," the crowd answered.

Dig's grandfather returned to the crowd.

Frank Lincroft, the family accountant, appeared at Dig's side. A sheen of sweat covered his bald head and his glasses had slipped down his nose. "How're you holding up Dig?"

Dig shrugged. "Okay I think. It's a lot to take in."

"Well, we're all here for you if you need anything."

"Cheers, Frank."

Frank bit at his lip. "Do you have a second to talk?"

Dig nodded.

Frank grabbed Dig's arm and pulled him away from the crowd. "I hate to bring this up now," Frank said. "But have you had any thoughts on what will happen to the brewery from here on in?"

Dig glanced over to where his brother was standing against the railing. He held a glowing cigarette and leaned against a post; his eyelids were heavy with whisky. "I guess we'll try to pick it up next week. Don't know how we'll organise it yet though."

Frank nodded. "Good." He took a sip of beer. "If you don't mind me asking, how are you with the brewing side of things? I know your father kept that pretty close to his chest."

Dig shrugged. "I've helped him out enough to know how to do it."

Frank leaned in close and whispered. "And what about these secret ingredients he imported from India? You got a handle on that? He wouldn't even tell me what they were..."

"Yeah, we know about them."

Frank nodded again. "Great," he said. "Because, well, I don't want to alarm you, but your father built the new brewery on the promise of some pretty large contracts, and the building itself is mortgaged heavily against the house." Frank met Dig's gaze. "It would be a good idea to get the brewery moving again as *soon as possible*, or your mother might just lose the family business and the family home."

Dig looked across to his mother as she spoke to his grandfather by the kitchen door. Her shoulders were stooped and a smear of mascara ran away from the corner of her eye.

"I hope I haven't said anything out of place," Frank said. "But, well, out of you and your brother, I think you're the one with the best chance of getting things back on track."

Dig took a deep breath. "Thanks for letting me know."

"No problem."

"Everyone!" Dig's brother slurred from the step above the crowd. He lifted a tumbler of whisky into the air, and a slosh of liquid spilled over the side. "Get yer' drinks up again."

The crowd hushed and sporadically raised their drinks.

"To a great man, my dad." Jake lifted his glass to his mouth and tipped it back.

"Hear hear," a deep voice answered from the rear of the group. The crowd murmured in agreement.

Jake swallowed and his lips thinned. "Just wish I could've been there that day. I wouldn't have let you die."

Silence filled the air, and Dig frowned. A flush rose into his cheeks. "What's that supposed to mean?" he said.

Dig's mother stepped forward. "It doesn't mean anything. He's just a little upset." She hooked her arm around Jake's shoulders and herded him back toward his position on the railing.

Jake shrugged her away and caught his balance against a table. "Of course I meant it!" he mumbled. "Dad was allergic to wasps. Why the hell didn't he—"

"Shut it!" his mother snapped, and Jake's mouth hung open.

Dig clenched his teeth and glanced around him. His neighbour dropped his eyes as he met Dig's gaze. Someone coughed at the back of the group.

Dig's shoulders tensed as he turned back to his mother. "No. Let him speak," he said. "I'd like to hear his opinion."

His mother shook her head. "I really don't think—"

"Are you saying Dad's death could have been avoided?"

Jake pushed a hand into his pocket. He suddenly seemed very interested in the cubes of ice in his empty glass, swirling them around in a circular rhythm.

Dig's forehead creased. "What are you saying Jake?"

Jake blinked, then finally lifted his head and gave a shrug. "You should've told Dad to take the needle," he said. "He'd be alive if you had." He reached behind him for the bottle of whisky and poured himself another helping, then replaced the bottle firmly on the wooden balustrade with a thunk. The cousins whispered to each other beside him.

Dig stared at his brother, breathing heavily. His vision doubled as tears welled in his eyes. His hands balled into fists and his nails dug into his palms. He wanted to shout. He wanted to fight. He wanted to punch his brother's nose so hard it bent halfway across his face.

But most of all, he wanted to get away.

The crowd parted as he stumbled toward the back steps. A tear tracked down his cheek and he wiped at it roughly with the back of his hand.

"Dig, wait!" his mother called after him.

He dropped down the steps into the backyard and cut around the corner of the house, then stopped abruptly as he nearly walked headlong into a standing ladder.

His heart sank as he recognised it. It was the same ladder his father had set up the week before, unmoved since the accident. Dig looked up to the gutter line, then stepped onto the first rung and began to climb. The ladder wobbled in his grasp.

When he reached the top he hoisted himself to the roof. The tiles were hard and jagged against his knees through the thin fabric of his suit pants. He crawled toward the chimney, then stopped beside the patch of fresh tiles that he and his father had placed the week before. He sat on the apex of the roof, and pulled his knees close to his body.

On the horizon, grey clouds tracked above the blanket of green trees. His gaze fixed on the waterhole.

Man I love the view up here, his father had said the week before. Dig pursed his lips and wiped the tears from his cheeks. An emptiness hung in his chest like a heavy weight.

His thoughts turned to his brother, and he slowly shook his head. Jake had always been an arsehole, but his words on the deck were inexcusable. How could he even bring himself to look at Jake again, let alone work with him to rebuild the family business?

A fluttering sound filled the air, and he turned to see a small multicoloured bird land on the top of the chimney beside a partially concealed nest. It lowered a grub into the twittering beak of a new hatchling, before preening itself and gliding away toward the deck.

A buzzing hum followed, and an insect rose over the line of the gutter toward him, dancing circles in the prevailing wind. It paused above him. Dig's breath caught in his throat.

It was a wasp.

The creature's dark eyes were ringed with a sick yellow. A blur of wings supported a bloated abdomen of black and yellow stripes, hanging heavily from its upper body.

Dig glared at the wasp. The insect represented everything that had gone wrong over the past week—the catalyst that had set the chain of bad events into action. Blood pounded in his ears.

"Piss off," Dig shouted, and swatted his hand at it. It ducked away in the breeze before darting back, shrill and angry. The buzzing was louder now, and it zigzagged through the air toward him.

"I said piss off! It's all your bloody fault!" He leaned forward with the action of an overhand tennis smash, concentrating all his energy into the strike.

He hit it hard, a satisfying thump against the centre of his palm. The wasp buffeted downward, bounced off a roof tile and disappeared over the line of the gutter.

"That's right." Dig lifted his chin. "And don't come back." He dropped back to his rear, pulled his knees toward him, and took a few deep breaths.

A burning spear of pain shot through his right elbow. He turned to see the wasp perched on his suit, its stinger piercing the fabric.

Dig frantically swiped at the insect with the back of his hand— throwing it into the air. He dropped to his knees and crawled quickly to the gutter. When he reached the ladder he hoisted his body over the edge and climbed down, two rungs at a time.

He hit the ground and jogged across the driveway—heading for the office located in the corner of the brewery. He pulled opened the door, jumped inside, and swung it firmly shut behind him.

After flicking a switch on the wall, an overhead bank of fluorescent lights flashed once, twice, then powered into a bright glow. Dig searched the stale air around him, sure that the wasp would be circling there, tormenting him. But there was nothing.

The office was a small room, dominated by a timber desk wedged tight against the wall. Papers and folders were strewn across the surface, and an old desktop computer sat in one corner. A faded calendar hung above the desk, marked up in blue pen with stock delivery dates and meetings. A black roller chair with cracked padding sat in the middle of the room. This space was his father's domain, and as Dig dropped into the seat it squealed in protest.

He peeled off his suit jacket and placed it on the desk, then rolled up his shirt sleeve and studied his arm. The sting mark was clearly visible, a throbbing pink volcano just below the point of his elbow. Now he'd seen it, he became more aware of the pain—a hot pulsing needle of discomfort.

"What next?" he said to the room, and leaned back in the seat, nursing his elbow, waiting for the pain to subside.

A strange flush of heat rose through his upper body and into his neck. Goose bumps broke out across his arms—making his hairs stand on end.

He released the top two buttons on his shirt, and flapped the collar. His midriff suddenly itched, and he scratched at it through the fabric.

When that brought little relief, he pulled the tail of his shirt out from his pants, and found his stomach was covered in blotchy patches of pink.

"No."

The flush of heat was in his head now, a constricting squeeze between his temples. He took a deep breath, but it caught it his lungs and he bent forward into a bout of coughing. He was alarmed that his lungs felt like they were at half capacity.

He looked back to his elbow, and saw that it had swollen further, a wide throbbing Michelin man arm from elbow to wrist.

"Crap!"

He stood up, and his vision began to swim. He reached down for the arm of the chair and held on until the room returned to focus.

After a moment, he pushed through the door, back out into the light. The sun seemed extraordinarily bright, and he shielded his eyes as he shuffled across the driveway to the main house. He turned the corner using the brickwork for support, and lumbered up the back steps to the deck.

Two elderly women stopped their conversation and watched him as he climbed the steps, before Dig's mother spotted him and marched over. "Dig!" she said. "Where'd you go?"

"Mum," he said, panting. "Did Dad...have any more of those needles?" He pulled up his shirt to reveal his arm, now a swollen pink mass from wrist to elbow. "I think...I'm allergic too."

His mother raised her hand to her mouth, and her eyes widened. "A wasp?"

Dig nodded.

"Quickly." She grabbed his good arm and dragged him through the crowd; eyes followed them as they passed through. When they entered the house she pushed him onto the couch. "Wait." She disappeared into the hallway and returned a short time later holding an Epinephrine needle. "Here," she said. "In the—"

"Thigh," Dig finished for her, and grabbed the needle. He fumbled with the catch, placed it over his leg, and pressed it down.

He felt a brief twinge as it pierced his skin and entered the muscle. Soon after, a burning sensation spread through the flesh. He wanted to pull away, but he gritted his teeth and forced himself to leave it in place. His heart rate and breathing increased, and a tingling sensation washed up through his body and took seat in his scalp.

His mother stared at him, open mouthed. "You okay?"

Dig struggled to think. The tingling dissolved away, but the throbbing in his arm remained. His breathing dropped back to a normal level. He nodded. "I think so."

"I'm calling an ambulance anyway." She disappeared into the kitchen. People crowded the doorway behind him, watching. Jake stood amongst them, a tumbler of whisky back in his grasp. As he met Dig's gaze he scowled and shook his head, then pushed his way back out to the deck.

Dig let his head fall back against the couch. The lounge room fan revolved in the ceiling above, throwing down a welcome wall of air. He closed his eyes.

The ambulance arrived shortly after, and as the paramedics walked through the front door, Dig recognised them as the same pair that had treated his father the week before.

"This is him?" said the bald man with the beer gut. His mother nodded. He stopped beside Dig and gave him a quizzical look. "We met last week, right?"

"Yeah."

The paramedic moved in close and studied his face, revealing a forest of dark hair up his nose. His deodorant smelled like leather.

"How're you feeling?"

Dig shrugged. "Better than twenty minutes ago."

The man lifted Dig's shirt and examined his arm, then placed a stethoscope on his chest. "A few deep breaths please." Dig did as he was told.

The man shuffled through his medical bag and came up with a new needle. "You've had an aggressive anaphylactic reaction to the wasp sting. This needle contains an antihistamine and something that will reduce the swelling." He grabbed hold of Dig's good arm and injected it into the shoulder muscle.

"You're the son?"

Dig nodded.

"Susceptibility to allergic reactions is hereditary," he said. "If you had left it much longer, well...I don't think I need to tell you what would have happened. But it looks like that Epinephrine needle saved your life."

Dig's mother pursed her lips and folded her arms across her chest. "Two stings," she said. "What are the odds."

Quite low, Dig thought. *If you chase the wasp down and try to kill it with your bare hands that is.*

"Yeah, crazy odds," he said instead.

4

DIG SPENT A NIGHT IN HOSPITAL under observation, but when the anaphylaxis didn't return, he was released early the next morning. His mother drove him back to the house.

As they arrived home, Dig stepped out of the car into an overcast morning. A plane droned somewhere behind the clouds. He stretched and yawned.

"Thanks for picking me up," he said.

"No problem," said his mother, smiling weakly. "You want some lunch?"

Dig's eyes fixed on the brewery. The roller door was cranked open. His brow furrowed. "Maybe later. I might head next door for a bit."

He walked across the drive and stopped at the entrance to the warehouse. The air was cool inside, and his footfalls on the concrete echoed softly in the open space. Tall shelves flanked either side of the doorway, packed with orange pallets of beer, ready for delivery.

The storage area opened into the heart of the brewery, the cluster of shiny metal structures that were used in the beer making process itself—triangular roller mills, circular mash tuns, brew kettles, fermentation tanks, and at the back, tallest of all, was the large cylindrical silo that held the fermented barley. This was the area where his father had spent most of his time—and Dig half expected him to walk around a corner with a tub of hops balanced over his shoulder, flick a few switches and fire the equipment up for a new batch.

But he didn't appear, and the equipment lay silent, taunting him—for every day it wasn't in use was another day the brewery would fall deeper behind in their orders, and another step closer to bankruptcy.

Dig kept walking, past the brewing equipment and storage silos to the rear of the warehouse, and stopped in front of a low rectangular room set in the far corner. This room was concrete lined, and the only access door was sealed and locked.

A keypad was fixed on the wall beside the doorway, and Dig reached up to type in a six digit code. The device emitted a high pitched beep and the door popped open. A wall of cold air rushed out at him, triggering a carpet of goosebumps on his arms. He stepped inside.

The room was capped by a low concrete ceiling and lit by ranks of bright fluorescent lights. Metal shelving covered the walls, packed from floor to ceiling with white plastic tubs.

Dig pulled out the nearest tub from the shelf to find it empty. The tub beside it was empty too, but the third was half full of pale orange flower buds. These were the hops, the ingredient in beer that offers antibacterial and preservative benefits, balances out the sweetness of the malt with bitterness, and adds floral aromas that are the major contributor to a beer's flavour.

Dig grabbed a handful of petals and held them up to his nose. The fragrance was bitter and yet sweetly citrus. His father's words came back to him.

These are the best hops in the world, without a doubt.

"Checking out the magic ingredient are we?" said his brother from behind him. Dig's shoulders tensed, and he dropped the petals to the ground.

Jake was still wearing yesterday's crumpled suit. The front tail of his shirt hung over his belt. His eyes were red and watery, and a crop of stubble covered his face.

"You look like shit," Dig said.

Jake raised his eyebrows. "Slept in the office. It wasn't too comfortable."

Dig retrieved the spilt hops from the floor. "You know where he got this stuff from?"

"The hops? Didn't he get them from India somewhere?"

"Yeah, but from *who* exactly? Like, a supplier?"

Jake shrugged. "No. You don't know?"

Dig shook his head. "Nope. Dad handled all the supplies."

"Well we better figure it out. I talked to Frank Lincroft last night. He says we have to get this place cranking at full steam pretty soon or Mum loses the house."

"I know." Dig turned his back and replaced the hops into the tub. "Well there isn't a lot left here in storage, so we need to get some more, soon." He moved down the row to check the contents of the remaining tubs.

Jake scratched at his face. "Look, about yesterday—"

"Forget it," said Dig. "I get it. You think I killed Dad."

"I didn't say that."

Dig turned and glared at him.

"What I said was—"

"You know what?" Dig's heart raced in his chest. "I don't actually *care* what you think anymore. So you may as well shut your mouth." He slammed a tub back into position with a rattle. "I'll tolerate being in the same building as you for the sake of this family, and this brewery Dad worked so hard to build. But don't flatter yourself if you think your opinion matters to anyone else but your self-centred, lazy-arsed self." Dig stormed to the door, his shoulder thumping against Jake as he walked through.

"Oh sorry your Highness!" Jake shouted. "I wouldn't want to offend Daddy's favourite son! Mr I'm so *fucking boring* I may as well eat a wasp for breakfast and top myself too! Well guess what? Daddy's not here anymore...so who are you going to suck up to now?"

Dig stopped and stared at his brother. His hands balled into fists and he started breathing hard. "You're dead," he said through clenched teeth, and ran at him.

Jake eyes widened and he held up his palms up. "Hey." He took two steps backwards into the cool room, but Dig was too fast and threw a wide hook at Jake's head. Jake saw it coming and ducked. Dig's fist caught the corner of the metal shelf behind him, ripping away the skin from his knuckle. A plastic tub tipped and fell to the ground, spilling hop petals across the floor. Jake tripped backwards over the tub and landed on his rear. Dig followed him down, dropping a knee into the side of his ribs with all of his weight.

Jake grunted with the impact, then swung an elbow upwards and caught Dig in the cheekbone. Dig's vision doubled and he fell sideways, but he punched downward as he dropped, and felt his fist connect with something soft and knobbly that he hoped was Jake's nose.

Dig fell to his hands and knees on the cold concrete floor. He tried to blink his vision into normality as something hard struck him square in the stomach. He dropped to his side, gasping for air.

Buzzz!

The reverberation of the office doorbell echoed through the warehouse. Dig glanced up as he tried to draw air into his lungs. Jake sat on his rear beside him, also breathing hard, his face locked in a grimace. One arm was wrapped across his torso, his hand clutching at his ribs. A trail of crimson blood tracked from a nostril to the corner of his chin.

Buzzzzz!

"Hello?" a voice echoed through the building.

Dig reached for a shelf and pulled himself roughly to his feet. His brother blinked, then did the same. They hobbled out of the room and across the warehouse to the front entrance. Jake wiped at his bloody face with his shirt sleeve as he moved.

Buzzzzz! "Anyone here?" said the voice, louder now.

They reached the roller door to see three men standing in the opening. Dig recognised them as the same Indian men that had visited the brewery on the morning of the funeral. They wore the same dark suits, pale business shirts, and ties. The man with the deep-set eyes stood in the centre of the trio with his thuggish friends flanking him—one with a bald, front-row-forward head, the other with a thick jaw and crooked teeth.

The brothers stopped before the men, still panting. The hem of Jake's pant leg was caught in his sock. He wiped at his nose again, adding a fresh smear of crimson to the back of his sleeve.

Dig's attention turned to the visitor's suits, then his own faded T-shirt and shorts. His cheek throbbed and crowded the sight in one eye. A trail of blood ran down his injured knuckle to the end of his finger.

The man looked from Dig to Jake. His forehead creased, and he shared a raised eyebrow with the bald-headed thug before giving the brothers a wide but unconvincing smile. "Hello," he said. "We're sorry to disturb you, but we felt we needed to visit again."

"Ok," Dig said. "No problem."

"Who's in charge here?"

Dig opened his mouth to speak, but Jake interjected.

"I am," Jake said. "I'm the older brother, and I'm taking over the running of Buckley's from now on." He held out his hand, and glanced at Dig from the corner of his eye. "How can I help?"

The man's eyes darted from Jake to Dig. "Okay..." he said. "My name is Shiv, and I represent the Banyan Brewery."

"Great," said Jake, and nodded. He pursed his lips and gave Dig another sideways glance. There was a brief silence.

Shiv lifted an eyebrow. "We are your hop supplier from India."

"Oh!" Jake said. "Great! Yes...well...actually Dig and I were just talking about you guys. Great hops those, best ever." He nodded again, then after a pause, gave a thumbs up. "Um, love your work," he said as a fresh trickle of blood dropped from his nostril. He wiped it away quickly. "Sorry," he said. "Allergies," and gave a strained smile.

"Thanks," Shiv said with a blank look on his face. "Would you mind if we came in? I hope we're not...interrupting?"

"No, of course not. Come into the office." Jake beckoned them toward the office meeting room, wincing as he clutched at his rib. They followed him inside.

Framed pictures hung on the walls of the room, depicting Dig's father brewing in the early years. A small sink sat in one corner, stacked with dirty coffee cups and greasy cutlery. A long timber table that normally dominated the room had been pushed against the wall. A rumpled blanket and pillow lay in the centre of the linoleum floor, and the reek of whisky infused body odour filled the space. Jake knelt down, balled the blanket and pillow up in his arms, and threw them to the base of the sink.

Dig took hold of the table and dragged it back to the centre of the room. As he moved it, he glanced down to see a line of white powder and a rolled up note on the table-top. He swore under his breath and glared at Jake, whose eyes widened before he leaned down and brushed them away to the floor with the back of his arm.

"Please, sit down." Jake hastily arranged plastic seats around the table.

The men dropped into the seats and Shiv laced his fingers together on the surface.

"So how can we help you guys?" Jake said.

Shiv attempted another smile before speaking. "Before the unfortunate passing of your father, we had a successful agreement with your company that lasted many years."

"Yes," Jake said. "And let me say that we appreciate that agreement, and intend to maintain it into the future."

Shiv nodded slowly. "May I ask, are you aware of the full extent of our past arrangement?"

Jake glanced at Dig. "Um...no."

"Well, maybe I should explain. In exchange for receiving our hops, we would pick up certain *packages* from your father every second month. Does that sound familiar?"

Jake scratched at the back of his neck. "No, sorry," he said. "Dad did all the material ordering...so you might have to fill us in on the details."

"He didn't mention any package he was keeping aside this month?"

"No."

Dig's eyes narrowed and a heavy feeling settled into his stomach as a memory came back to him—a memory of his father lying stricken on the bush track, struggling to speak: *Tell...Max...the deal is off. No...more...packages.*

"No more packages," Dig said, and everyone turned to look at him. Jake frowned.

"Do you work for someone called Max?"

"That's correct."

"Well Dad did say something about the packages, right before he died. He said tell Max there are no more, and that the deal is off."

Shiv's lips pursed. "Are you sure of that?"

A flush rose in Dig's cheeks and he shifted in his seat. "Look, I'm just repeating what he said. I don't know the history behind all this. You seem like nice guys and all, but you may have Buckley's of getting that package you're after."

Shiv frowned. "What does this mean—*Buckley's*?"

"It's an Australian saying. *Buckley's Chance*—it means bugger all chance...pretty much none."

Shiv's jaw clenched and he exchanged a whispered conversation with the bald-headed thug.

A shoe thumped into Dig's ankle. He felt his brother's glare from beside him, but Dig wouldn't meet his eye. The three men continued to talk amongst themselves. While he waited, Dig took a closer look at them.

Shiv's suit was clean and well presented, but something didn't seem right. His shirt was a sky blue business model, and while it seemed new, it had defined creases running through it. In fact, the creases seemed to be spaced across the fabric in a rectangular grid.

That shirt is fresh out of the box, Dig thought.

The collar of the shirt sat high on Shiv's neck, but it failed to cover the top of a dark circular tattoo that was etched into the skin. Dig leant back to catch a glimpse of Shiv's feet. The shoes were brand new, shiny and black, but he wore no socks. A feeling of unease took hold in his chest.

Jake rose from his seat. "Hey, Shiv. Don't listen to him, he isn't running this show. The deal is *still on* guys. We'll get you whatever packages you need. Just tell us what you want."

Dig blinked rapidly, and grabbed Jake's arm. "I'm not sure if—"

"Please," Shiv motioned to the table. "Sit down."

Jake paused, then sat back down.

A realisation dawned in Dig's mind—and the unease in his chest began to rise up his windpipe. "So guys," he said in a stilted tone. "I didn't see you at the funeral. You couldn't make it?"

Shiv's eyes were cold. "We apologise but we were busy yesterday."

"Sure," Dig said. "Busy breaking into our house?" The words were out of his mouth before he had time to consider them.

The corners of Shiv's mouth rose slightly, and he leaned back in his seat. He took a deep breath, then reached for the knot of his tie and loosened it. When it was undone, he dropped into a curled heap on the table. He then released the top button of his shirt, letting the collar fall away from his neck to reveal more of the tattoo—a fire breathing dragon.

"I hate ties," Shiv said. "Feels like you're being choked." He tilted his head and poked out his tongue, then held an imaginary rope above his head and made a retching sound, before smiling.

Dig's stomach knotted, and he glanced at his brother.

"Your father was a good man. We could rely on him to be honest and do what he was told." Shiv drummed his fingers on the table. "But now? Well I'm disappointed. I'm looking at two hopheads who seem incapable of taking care of themselves, let alone become competent business partners."

"No," Jake said. "No way, you've got that wrong—"

"Really? Please, just take a look at each other."

Jake swallowed. "Listen, you've caught us at a bad time..."

Shiv stood up, and his companions rose with him.

"We can keep the deal going, just give us a chance."

Shiv shook his head, and gave another unbalanced smile. "You won't be hearing from us again."

"Whoah." Jake stood and gripped the edge of the table. "Not so fast. Our father's funeral was *yesterday*. You need to give us some time to get this place moving again. I'm sure we can figure something out. Just tell us how much you want for your hops. We've got some big contracts riding on those things. We can pay."

Shiv turned to his colleagues. "Let's go."

"No!" Jake shouted. He was breathing hard now, shoulders wide, with his fists clenched. He stepped forward, and the thugs turned their attention to him. "Don't you understand? You're screwing with our lives here. We *need* your hops to produce our beer, or this whole place will go under."

"Jake," Dig said. "Let's just calm down a bit."

"I have been calm! But these guys need to listen." He turned back to Shiv. "Now, if you would please just *sit down*, we can come to a proper deal on this."

Shiv's unbalanced smile returned. "Let me explain this in a way that you might actually understand," he said. "You have...*Buckley's* of making any deal happen." He cocked his eyebrows and turned to Dig. "Did I say that right?" His colleagues chuckled behind him.

Jake took the final few strides toward Shiv like a charging bull and took hold of Shiv's upper arm. "You aren't going anywhere buddy," he seethed, and a dab of spittle shot from his mouth and landed on Shiv's chin.

The bald-headed thug bounded across the room, surprisingly quick for his size, and hooked an arm around Jake's neck, yanking him backwards. Jake struggled against the man with his teeth clenched—his fingertips disappeared into the fabric of Shiv's suit arm. "You think you can break into our house," he shouted. "Then just waltz in here and laugh about it? I think it's time we called the cops." He pulled hard on Shiv's arm and toppled him backwards to the ground, where he landed awkwardly on his side. Shiv gritted his teeth before turning back to Jake with his nostrils flared and eyes like pinpricks.

The thug dragged Jake backwards across the room with his arms and legs flailing.

"Leave him!" Dig shouted, and threw himself at the thug, driving his shoulder into his ribcage. The thug grunted and buckled slightly, but remained upright. Dig fell to the floor.

Shiv brushed at his suit with his lips thin, then pulled himself to his feet. "Put him on the table," he said. The thug dragged Jake toward the table and pushed him down, face first, then twisted his arm behind his back.

"Get off me!" Jake shouted, and tried to wrench away from his grasp.

"He can watch," Shiv said. A hand yanked Dig sideways by the collar of his shirt and dragged him across the floor—the material dug into his chin. Dig managed a breath before he was lifted and slammed forward onto the table.

His brother's face was beside him, etched in fear. "What are you doing?" Jake said in a high, strained voice. "Let us go."

Shiv extracted a serrated metal knife from the sink, and studied it. "Do you have anything sharper?" He ran his finger across the blade, then crouched down beside Jake at eye level. "I'm sure you'd prefer a clean cut." He shrugged before dimpling Jake's cheek with its point. "But it seems this will have to do."

Jake's face was pale and his bottom lip trembled. "Look," he said. "I may have overstepped the mark a bit. You can go now, and we'll forget about everything."

Shiv smiled. "I don't think you'll be forgetting this." He nodded to the bald-headed thug, who yanked Jake's arm to the tabletop. Shiv plucked his abandoned tie from the table and fastened an end tightly around Jake's wrist, then tied the other end to the table leg. Jake buckled and pulled at the tie, but he couldn't escape the binding. The thug forced Jake's palm down hard onto the table, inches away from Dig's nose.

Shiv placed the blade between Jake's ring and pinky fingers. Before Dig had a chance to look away, Shiv began sawing rapidly back and forth through the joint of the pinky with a ripping, crunching sound.

Jake thrashed and bellowed. *"Stop! My fi—Oh Chr—!"* His knee pounded against the table leg, the table skipping forward across the floor with each impact.

Dig retched, and tried to subdue the surge of vomit climbing into his throat.

Shiv continued to saw until the blade dropped to the table with a thunk. He lifted the knife and the finger rolled away, revealing a cross section of pink flesh and cartilage, and a stream of blood that pulsed out of the wound, creating an expanding crimson circle on the table top that crept closer and closer toward Dig's face. He clenched his teeth and jammed his eyes shut.

"No," said a voice in his ear. "You watch!" The point of the knife pressed into his ribs. He glanced sideways. Shiv crouched beside him; his breath smelled of stale cigarettes. "This is what happens if you don't listen," he said. "Look at him."

"Let me up!" Dig panted.

"Nobody calls the cops...right?"

Dig nodded quickly, his eyes locked on the blood advancing across the timber surface. It was within inches of his face now, a thick oozing fluid. Dig bucked against the weight on his back, trying to break free. A wailing moan rumbled in his throat.

"Otherwise, we take another finger. Next time it will be your mother's. After that, we take your ear. Understand?"

"Yes!" Dig whimpered. "We'll keep quiet. Please...let me up."

But they didn't let him up, and the blood pooled outward to reach Dig's face, a sickening liquid warmth that first encircled the tip of his nose, then seeped into his nostril with a slippery metallic stink. Dig's stomach clenched, and he choked sour vomit onto the table-top.

The weight on the back of Dig's head released, and he scrambled away from the table, falling to his backside on the floor. He wiped madly at his face.

His brother sat on the floor beside him, cradling his arm. His pants leg was dark and wet, and the stench of urine hung the air. "My finger!" he sobbed. "You fuckers cut it off!"

Shiv stood over them, flanked by his colleagues. "Yes," he said, and reached to the table-top to pick up the digit. The nail on the finger was visible, and quite short. Jake had always been partial to biting them. "Max will want this." Shiv held it up with a wrinkled nose. He prised a square of paper towel loose from a dispenser above the sink, and wrapped the finger neatly inside.

Jake moaned. His shirt was covered in blood. "I'm going to die!"

Shiv smirked. "You'll live. Take my word for it." He held up a hand, and Dig noticed for the first time that his pinky finger was missing; a web of lumpy scar tissue lay in its place. Shiv nodded to his friends, and they walked out of the room.

Dig reached for the table and pulled himself to his feet, then yanked a tea towel from the sink and threw it to his brother. Jake wrapped it around his hand and it immediately soaked red with blood.

"We better get to the hospital."

5

"I JUST DON'T UNDERSTAND HOW someone just *loses* a finger!" Dig's mother stood in the doorway to the hospital room, holding a curled fist to her mouth. A nurse wheeled a bed through the corridor behind her. "I mean, you must have seen where it went."

Jake lay on the bed with his hand propped up and wrapped in a bandage. His eyes were puffy; he was still groggy from the operation. "Mum I told you," he croaked. "I was washing out the fermentation tank and the lid dropped down on my hand. By the time I could think straight enough to realise my finger was gone, it had washed down the drain with the rest of the liquid."

"So what did the doctors do?"

Dig sat beside Jake on a plastic chair. "They cleaned it up and closed the wound with some skin from his thigh. That's the best they could do in the circumstance."

Jake cleared his throat. "They should've taken the skin from the couple of toes I've got webbed together. You know, sort out the Buckley deformity while they were at it."

Genetic advancement, Dig thought.

"You poor thing." She stepped forward to brush the hair away from Jake's eyes. "Well at least you're still in one piece." Her cheeks blushed pink. "I mean...that you are *okay.*" She dropped her head and straightened the sheets of Jake's bed.

Jake rolled his eyes and stared at the wall.

"You boys have got to be more careful," she continued. "I don't want any more surprises right now, or I just might have...a nervous breakdown or something." She finished rearranging the sheets and looked back to Jake. "Is there anything I can get you?"

"Could you ask about some more pain relief?"

"No problem," she said, patting his free hand. "I'll get a nurse." She turned and walked out of the room.

Dig scratched at his ear. "How're you feeling then?"

"Been better."

He took a glance out to the corridor. "Should we at least *consider* getting the cops involved?"

"And hide for the rest of our lives? Not likely. Even if we caught those guys we'd be waiting for more to turn up. And I get the feeling the cops might be interested in those packages Dad gave them over the last few years."

Dig shook his head. "What about swapping the hops? Or we try to make a better beer?"

"We can't change the recipe. The contracts are for Buckley's Chance, nothing else. And Dad mixed up crap recipes for twenty years before getting it right. We don't have a hope in trying another one."

Dig leaned back in his seat and hooked his hands behind his head. "There must be a way to sort this out."

"There's no way. We're screwed, that's all there is to it. I don't know what kind of arrangement Dad had with those gangsters, but whatever it was, it's gone. And as soon as our hop supplies run out, Buckley's Chance will die as well—and take the whole brewery down with it." Jake sighed. "I think we need to tell Mum."

"No." Dig folded his arms. "Not yet. Just give me a day to think about it."

When he returned home, Dig headed to the brewery office. He dropped into the revolving metal chair and spun himself around, thinking.

They were stuck between two bad options. If they accepted the current situation and tried to continue on, the brewery faced certain ruin. All their major contracts relied on the imported hops, and if those contracts defaulted, there would be no turning the business around.

Alternatively, they could try to salvage a working relationship with a bunch of people who seemed not only intentionally mysterious, but downright psychotic.

Dig sighed, then turned his attention to the desk in front of him. The dusty desktop computer sat against the wall. A plastic in-tray sat beside it, filled with a messy pile of papers. Dig lifted the top piece of paper from the tray—an invoice for cardboard packaging. He placed it to one side and continued through the pile. He found what he was looking for about halfway through the papers, and held the crumpled page up to the light.

INVOICE

Banyan Breweries
Hampi 583227
PO Box 5089
(+91) 09 242 641559

Invoice No.	72435
Date:	7th Sept
Due Date:	7th Oct

Description	Amount
50 kg Dried Hops	$2,000
50 kg Dried Hops	$2,000
50 kg Dried Hops	$2,000
50 kg Dried Hops	$2,000
50 kg Dried Hops	$2,000
Customs Shabdkosh	$2,350
Bay-Ta Brewing Yeast	$5,000
Net Amount Due:	**$17,350**

Preferred Payment Method - Direct Bank Transfer
Bank: Canara Bank
Branch: Hampi
IFCS Code: CNRB0001187
Account: 0154563

He leaned back in the seat, invoice in hand, and spun around again in a slow revolution while he considered his options. After a few moments, he returned his attention to the paper and studied the details in the top corner.

Phone: (+91) 09 242 641559

Dig glanced to the phone sitting in its cradle, then reached out and picked it up. The hum of a dial tone droned in his ear. He checked the invoice and punched the numbers into the keypad.

After a few clicks and hisses, a muffled ring echoed down the line. It rang a few times before it was answered.

"Hello," said a voice in an unmistakable Indian accent.

"Oh hello," Dig said. "I was wondering if I could speak to Max please."

There was a pause. "Yes, this is Max."

"Oh hi. My name's Dig Buckley. I think that you may know...um...may have *known* my father, Shaun Buckley?"

The hush of static filled the line. "What is the purpose of your call?"

"Well, I'm guessing you already know this, but we had some bad news this week regarding my father. He was involved in an accident and has died."

A pause. "Yes."

"Well, my brother and I are trying to pick up the areas of the business my father controlled, including delivery of materials such as your hops. We had a meeting with one of your guys this week, a guy called Shiv. Does that sound right?"

There was no answer.

"Look, I don't know if you've heard yet, but unfortunately our meeting with Shiv didn't go too well. I'm calling to try to put that meeting behind us, and continue our previous hop supply arrangement from your company."

The static crackled in the line, and ran for an uncomfortably long period of time.

"Max?" Dig said. "You there?"

"Don't ring here again," said the voice. The line clicked, and the monotonous pulse of the engaged signal filled his ear.

"Crap!" Dig stared at the phone for a few moments, then checked the invoice and punched the numbers into the keypad again. The phone rang with three long rings, before the line dropped immediately into the engaged tone.

"Crap, Crap, Crap!" Dig slammed the phone back into its cradle. He kicked away from the desk, and the chair rolled across the room.

He tried to ring four more times that day. The first three times the line went dead before he had a chance to say a word. The fourth time he rang as a hidden number on his mobile phone, but when the phone was finally answered, he only got out the word "Hello?" before the line went dead once again.

His mother found him the next morning, sitting back in the office chair, staring at the ceiling. He held the invoice in his hand. The computer screen glowed bright in front of him.

"Here you are."

Dig took an intake of breath and turned quickly at her voice. Bags hung under his red eyes. "Oh," he said. "You scared me."

She folded her arms. "You've been in here all night?"

"Something like that."

She frowned. "Well it's time you came out. I'm going back to see Jake. You coming?"

Dig stretched and yawned, then nodded.

They didn't speak on the way into the hospital. His mother drove with her head tilted to one side and a small plastic container balanced on her lap. Dig stared forward at the road.

When they arrived, they found Jake lying flat on his back, his head propped up with two pillows, staring up at a small television bolted to the ceiling. His face was covered in stubble and his hair was greasy. He glanced at them as they entered, then returned his attention to the low hum of the screen.

"Hi Jake. How are you doing?" Dig's mother said in a soothing tone.

He gave a small shrug.

She pulled a seat to the side of the bed and sat down. Dig stood inside the doorway. "I have a present." She handed him the plastic container. "I made you some biscuits."

Jake glanced at the container with a blank look. "Thanks."

"So how is the...hand?"

"Sore." He looked back up at the television.

"Oh you poor thing. Don't worry, we'll get you home soon, and you can have a solid rest for a few days to recuperate." She reached out and tried to adjust Jake's hair, but he ducked away from her reach. "And don't worry, Dig can run the brewery till you're back on your feet. I might even get in there and help a bit. What do you think Dig? Want me to haul a few sacks of barley to help get things moving?"

"Humph," Jake said, his eyes not leaving the screen. "Not likely."

"Come on. It's not all that bad."

Jake raised his eyebrows at Dig, and Dig dropped his gaze to the floor. The voice of the television news anchor-man chattered in the background, discussing the previous night's cricket score.

"Mum," Jake said. "We've got something important we need to tell you."

Her eyebrows furrowed as she looked back and forth between her sons. "What?" she said. "What is it?" Her hand grasped tightly at the strap of her purse.

Jake sighed. "Mum, it looks like—"

"That I'm going to India," Dig interjected.

They turned to stare at him.

Dig stood stiffly. "Yes," he said as he scratched at his neck. "I'm going to India...to meet up with our hop suppliers. Nothing to worry about, just a face-to-face to maintain the business relationship now Dad isn't about."

"Oh," said Dig's mother. "That's...interesting news."

Jake pursed his lips. "Yes," he said. "Very interesting." He pushed himself upright in the bed. "Mum? Would you mind getting me a good coffee from downstairs? The stuff they serve here is shit."

Her eyes narrowed, and she looked back and forth between her sons. "Everything alright?"

"Of course," Jake rubbed his ear. "Just need a good caffeine fix, that's all."

She sighed and walked out of the room.

Jake waited until the click clack of her heels had receded far enough down the hall before speaking. "You're kidding right?" he whispered.

"No."

"But that guy's a lunatic!"

"Yes," Dig said. "But he isn't the one who runs the operation—this Max character does. If I can just talk to him, then maybe we can sort this problem out."

"Not going to happen."

Dig raised his eyebrows. "Oh *okay*," he said, walking forward to the edge of Jake's bed. "Then let's just tell Mum that after one week of taking over the brewery that we've managed to ground it to a halt and push it into bankruptcy...and oh, by the way Mum, you better start packing up your stuff—as you won't have the house much longer either!"

Jake's head dropped. "Well if you're so keen to talk to this Max guy, then why don't you just ring him?"

Dig swallowed. "I did. And he keeps hanging up on me...but before you say anything, I think that if I can just get a chance to meet him face-to-face, and explain things calmly, then we might just be able to turn things around."

"Have you ever considered that maybe we don't *want* to turn things around? Dad apparently told you the *deal is off*. Why the hell would he say that? Why would he intentionally destroy the one beer that keeps the brewery ticking?"

Dig pushed his hands into his pockets. "Yes, I was thinking about that last night. And no, I can't understand it." He bit at his lip. "But you know, maybe he was delusional and didn't know what he was saying..."

Jake's voice raised an octave. "Maybe he was *delusional?* Now you suddenly doubt your spectacular deathbed confession?"

Dig pulled a piece of paper from his pocket and dumped it on the bed sheet.

"Look."

INVOICE

Banyan Breweries
Hampi 583227
PO Box 5089
(+91) 09 242 641559

Invoice No.	72435
Date:	7th Sept
Due Date:	7th Oct

Description	Amount
50 kg Dried Hops	$2,000
50 kg Dried Hops	$2,000
50 kg Dried Hops	$2,000
50 kg Dried Hops	$2,000
50 kg Dried Hops	$2,000
Customs Shabdkosh	$2,350
Bay-Ta Brewing Yeast	$5,000
Net Amount Due:	$17,350

Preferred Payment Method - Direct Bank Transfer
Bank: Canara Bank
Branch: Hampi
IFCS Code: CNRB0001187
Account: 0154563

Jake glanced at the paper and shrugged. "An invoice. So what?"

Dig leaned forward and pointed to at an item on the list. "Bay-ta Brewing Yeast. It's on all the Banyan invoices."

Jake shrugged. "And?"

"Well first, we don't use that type of yeast. We use the local liquid stuff. And second, this yeast was never delivered. Not on *any* of the deliveries. I know, because I unpacked the Banyan containers myself." Dig shook his head. "Why would we be charged for something we never received?"

Jake blinked. "Who fucking cares? It's over. Let it go."

"Don't you want to know what it's all about?"

"Dig, these people are *not normal*—they chopped my finger off just because I raised my voice."

"It was a little more than that—"

"I don't care! You can't fix this! Once again you think that you can do something *better* than me. That just because you were Dad's best mate you can make decisions for us all. But this time you're just going to get yourself killed."

Dig glared at his brother. "Bloody hell," he seethed. "This isn't about me being better than you. What's your problem? Don't you want to sort this out?"

Jake fell back against his pillow and stared at the television. "Whatever," he said. "Just do what you want. If you want to die, then go right ahead."

Dig walked to the side of the bed. His hands were shaking and his nerves felt like raw electrical wires; his eyes were red raw from lack of sleep. "We don't always have to work against each other you know."

Jake continued to stare at the television.

"What is it Jake? Like, I know you're an arsehole, but this week you're off the charts."

Jake closed his eyes and his forehead creased. For a long time, the voice of the television anchor-man was the only sound that filled the room.

"What is it?" Dig repeated.

Jake blinked and moisture welled in the corner of his eye. "It doesn't matter," he said in a quiet voice.

"Just tell me!"

Jake pursed his lips and dropped his gaze. After a long moment he spoke in the same dull tone. "I didn't help him."

"Who?"

"Dad." Jake's bottom lip quivered. "He asked me to help him fix the roof, but I pretended I had to work." He swallowed and a tear dropped down the side of his face. "But *you* helped him. And *you* got to say goodbye."

"I got him killed you mean."

Jake rolled his eyes. "I shouldn't have said that. I was angry at myself more than anything, and I took it out on you."

Dig thought back to the day of the wake, to the crowd staring at him as Jake accused him of being responsible for his father's death. It was an almost unforgivable act. But, for the good of them both, he had to try.

He took a deep breath. "Okay," he said. "Let's just forget about it."

"I'm sorry, if it makes any difference."

Dig shrugged. His brother seemed deflated, a shell of his normal bolshy self. "We all have stuff that we regret about that day. But we can't change it. We need to forget about the past for now and just channel our energy into trying to get this brewery moving again."

Jake hauled himself upright in his bed. "Look," he said. "If you really want to go to India, then do it. But just don't get sliced up okay? We can't afford to lose you too."

Dig reached out and grabbed Jake's hand. "I hear you."

Jake pulled his hand away. "Hey, no need to get all bent on me." He wiped at his face and threw back the covers. "I think it's also time I left this germ farm. Someone's got to handle the orders while you're gone." He dropped his legs over the edge of the bed and winced as the thigh that had been used for the skin graft took some weight. "But for the record, that sham of a gangster already said you've got Buckley's of sorting anything out over there."

Dig shrugged. "Buckley's chance is better than no chance at all."

When they returned home, Dig packed a few clothes and toiletries into a small daypack, and called a taxi for the airport. He didn't want to waste any more time at home, because he feared if he took another night to think about it, he may lose his courage to leave at all.

He walked out to the front drive, waiting for the taxi to arrive. His brother followed him out and stood beside him, then pointed to Dig's pack with his bandaged hand. "Packing light?"

"I don't plan to be there long. You going to be okay back here?"

"There's enough stock on the shelves for about a week. I'll fill the outstanding orders with what we have. But after that, all bets are off."

"I'll be back in a week."

"Well...give us a call at some point huh?"

Dig nodded.

The taxi arrived and pulled into the drive. As Dig reached for the door, his mother called from the steps of the house. She strode across the drive, then held out two Epinephrine needles. "I'm sure there are wasps in India too." She gave him a hug.

Dig hugged her back, then tucked the needles into the side pocket of his pack. He opened the door of the taxi and settled into the back seat. The driver clunked the vehicle into drive, and it pulled out, heading for the airport.

6

IT WAS THE EARLY HOURS OF THE MORNING, and the lights were dim in the cabin of the plane. A man with long curly hair slept beside Dig, his mouth open wide, snoring in his ear. Dig sat under a solitary reading light, flicking restlessly through a copy of the in-flight magazine. He returned to look at the map of India on the inside cover. A small star on the western edge of the country was marked *Mumbai: Population 12 million.* His stomach felt queasy as he removed the folded invoice from his pocket and studied the address in the top corner:

Banyan Brewery
Hampi 583227
PO Box 5089

It showed a postal box in the town of Hampi, which according to the internet, was eight hundred kilometres inland from Mumbai. After the fourteen-hour flight, he needed to find a bus to take him overland.

The cabin lights flickered and the engine changed pitch, adjusting into a descent. Dig bit his lip and replaced the paper into his pocket.

The plane touched down at Mumbai airport at 7:15 a.m. A bleary-eyed group of passengers queued through the visa counters and collected their luggage from the carousels. Two armed guards flanked the doors that separated the air conditioned airport lobby from the outside world. Dig threw his pack over his shoulder and nodded to the men as he passed through.

When he stepped outside, a haze of humidity overwhelmed him—infused with car exhaust and stagnant stormwater. His arms quickly lined with sweat.

A line of taxis with yellow roofs queued on a potholed road. On the kerb, men in dark pants and collared shirts held up signs: Mr Stoddart, Mr Andrade, and Mr Hangapasharang.

"Taxi sir?" A man stood at his shoulder in a faded blue uniform.

"I'm trying to get to Hampi," Dig said. "Can you take me to the bus terminal?"

"Of course."

Dig dropped into the rear seat. A vent in the dash blew a stream of warm air into his face. The vehicle pulled away from the kerb and jerked up through the gears. As they joined the freeway traffic, Dig pulled his pack to his chest and watched the scenery flash past the window: boys cycling rickety bikes down the pavement; men crouched on street corners selling newspapers; children sifting through piles of rubbish beside an active food stall; a man sleeping in a rickshaw with a mangy dog on his lap. Dig took in the images with his eyes wide and a flutter in his stomach.

A large advertising billboard stood high on the side of the road. It depicted a group of friends sitting around a table with drinks in their hands, laughing. An image of a green labelled beer bottle featured prominently beside the picture with the words *Banyan Bitter* emblazoned across it in yellow. A slogan ran across the base of the advertisement:

Banyan Bitter—Bringing Friends Together

Dig sat up straight, then leaned forward to the driver. "Excuse me," he said, pointing up at the sign. "Is that beer popular? Banyan Bitter?"

The driver wobbled his head. "Yes, it's sold right down the coast."

Dig nodded and retrieved his phone from the front pocket of his backpack. He fired off a quick picture from the camera before returning it to the bag. The driver watched him from the rear view mirror.

The taxi turned off the freeway into a hazy concrete courtyard crowded with buses and people. The driver pointed to a dusty bus with faded panelling parked at the far end of the clearing. "Bus to Hampi."

"Thanks." Dig removed a note from his wallet. "Are you okay with a thousand rupee note? It's all I could get from the airport machine."

"Yes, I have change." The driver took the money and counted some bills into his hand, then exited the cab to scoot around and open Dig's door. Dig stepped onto the pavement while shielding his eyes from the sun. The crowd jostled past his shoulder, heading into the terminal.

"Enjoy your trip," the driver shouted.

"Thanks." Dig joined the crowd.

Restaurants lined the perimeter of the courtyard, where men sat at low tables and ate lumpy yellow rice with their hands. A cow with a rack of protruding ribs walked casually past the diners and emptied its bowels. The men seemed unconcerned as the shop owner retrieved a broom and swept the deposit out into the pavement.

An elderly man appeared at Dig's elbow, hobbling, and tugged at his shirt sleeve. His left eye was a sunken hole; the other eye was clouded in cataract. The man clutched fingers to his mouth, demonstrating his hunger.

Dig fished in his pockets and found a solitary ten rupee coin, which he handed over. But the man didn't leave. Instead he walked with extra vitality, tugging harder at his sleeve as Dig continued across the terminal. Dig increased his stride, but the man matched his speed in a looping, unbalanced gait.

At his other elbow, two children in faded clothes now kept pace and held their hands outstretched. Dig turned his pockets inside out, but they continued to tug at his shirt until he reached the bus.

Passengers crowded against the vehicle, their possessions wrapped in balls of fabric or stacked in cardboard boxes. Dig joined the moshpit, and hands in his back shoved him forward through the door opening.

Inside, the ceiling was low, and Dig ducked as he moved down the aisle. A stink of motor oil and body odour hung in the air. He was lucky to snag a berth on a flat steel bench at the rear of the bus.

An elderly woman wrapped in a brown sari pressed against his left shoulder. The baby on her lap watched him with large eyes. A middle aged man smelling of tobacco pressed against his right, a forest of grey hairs growing from his ear. The seat in front of Dig felt impossibly close, and he propped one leg up against it. As the bus pulled away from the kerb a numbing tingle started in his rear and worked its way up his hamstring.

The bus stopped often on the way out of town, and with each stop, more passengers squashed into the aisle. A young conductor sidled up to them and took notes from them in a silent understanding. When he reached Dig he looked him up and down. "Where you going?"

"Hampi. How much is that?"

"Fourteen hundred."

Dig counted out the bills.

The boy examined a few of the notes and returned them to him. "Fake."

Dig blinked. "Huh?"

"Fake notes." He pulled a genuine bill from his pocket and held it out. The paper was softer and the ink sharper.

Dig thought back to the taxi driver and his cheeks flushed warm. "Right." He handed over a larger note and the boy returned some change to him.

A nagging unease hung with him as the conductor moved further down the aisle. After a moment he pulled his bag to his lap and examined the front zipper. The pocket was open. His phone was gone. He remembered the driver helping him out of the taxi and clenched his teeth.

Great, he thought. *I've only been here thirty minutes and I've been ripped off twice.*

He already felt alone and defenseless in the new country, but now the emergency link to his family had been taken, he felt more isolated than ever.

It's just a phone, he told himself, but the unsettling churn in his stomach did not dissipate.

The bus pulled away from the kerb, and Mr Hairy Ears fell asleep beside him. With each bump in the road, his head lolled and bounced off Dig's shoulder.

Dig took a deep breath and checked his watch. Another thirteen hours to travel through the night. He hugged his bag to his chest and willed the time to pass.

He drifted in and out of a nocturnal haze until the sunrise lifted over the horizon to reveal a series of rocky mountains. As the bus laboured over the crest of a hill it slowed, then pulled into the dirt shoulder with a flurry of gravel against the undercarriage, and stopped.

Outside the window, a cluster of police stood behind a set of timber barriers. A young policeman stepped through the door and barked an order in Hindi. The passengers retrieved their luggage and made their way forward off the bus.

Dig turned to Mr Hairy Ears. "Are we there? Hampi?"

The man shook his head. "Police check."

Dig grabbed his pack and pulled himself to his feet. He tried to massage some life into his legs as he limped down the aisle, then squinted into the early morning sun as he stepped off the bus.

The passengers stood in a ragged line on the road shoulder with their possessions piled around their feet. A burly policeman in a black peaked cap moved down the line and sifted through the possessions, requesting bags and boxes to be opened for inspection.

Dig turned to Hairy Ears. "What are they looking for?"

"Anything illegal." He shrugged. "You know...drugs, alcohol, guns."

"Alcohol's illegal?"

He nodded, scratching at his jaw. "Hampi's a holy city. Alcohol is banned."

"Okay."

The policeman lifted a bottle of wine from the pack of a guy with oily dreadlocks, and thrust it into his face, shouting. The guy stood stiffly with his hands clasped together, before a junior policeman grabbed the guy's upper arm and dragged him away.

The head policeman sauntered down the line until he reached Dig. He chewed gum as he looked him up and down, then motioned at Dig's pack. Dig held it open. The policeman sifted through the bag before giving a small nod. He pointed toward the bus, and Dig returned to his seat beside Hairy Ears.

"We escaped," Dig said.

Hairy Ears smiled and nodded. The bus pulled back out to the road and continued its journey.

Shortly after, square concrete buildings began to crowd both sides of the road. The bus turned into a wide piece of dirt lined with shops and market stalls, and came to a lumbering halt at a crowded steel shelter. Inside the bus, the passengers stood and began pushing toward the door.

Hairy Ears stood beside Dig, holding a cardboard box to his chest. He turned to Dig. "Hampi," he said.

Dig smiled. "Great, thanks."

7

DIG STEPPED DOWN FROM THE BUS and pushed through the crowd, trying to shake out the remaining stiffness in his legs. Children dodged past him, chasing each other down the dusty road. A vendor tried to beckon him into a clothing stall. The tall spine of an ancient looking temple stood at the end of the street. In the distance, pointed hills lined up across the horizon, covered in boulders of orange stone.

On his left was a dusty shopfront with a crooked sign in the window stating *Helpful Hari's Tourist Information*. Dig ducked through a curtain of amber beads hanging in the doorway.

A man with a crooked tie and bushy sideburns sat behind a counter. A girl with blonde hair and sunburnt arms stood in front of him, paging through a brochure. "I think I'll go on the boat tour," she said.

"Excellent," the man said. "It leaves at 2 p.m. That'll be six hundred rupees." The girl handed over some cash and he wrote out a receipt. "See you at two." She left the room.

The man turned to Dig. "Hello Sir! I'm Hari. Where are you from?"

"Australia."

"Ah, Steve Smith and David Warner. Good Australian cricketers."

"Yeah. They're pretty good."

"David Warner is playing for the Sunrisers tonight in the Indian Premier League. You watching?"

"I wouldn't mind, but I don't think I'll have time. Has Dhoni retired yet?"

"Yes, unfortunately he has. India will miss him." Hari brought his hands together in front of him. "So, how can I help?"

"Well," Dig said. "I'm looking for a business in Hampi called the Banyan Brewery. Do you know where that is?"

Hari frowned and stroked the loose fold of skin under his chin.

A clattering interrupted them as a stocky, bearded man wearing a creased suit pushed through the wall of beads. Hari gave him a subtle nod then turned to Dig. "Please wait a moment." He moved to the end of the counter and started a whispered conversation. Hari produced a well-worn notebook from beneath the table, scribbled on a slip and exchanged it for a bundle of notes. The stocky man ducked his head and turned back out into the street.

"I'm sorry about that," Hari said. "Now, what was the business called again?"

"The Banyan Brewery."

He shook his head. "No. I've never heard of that business."

"Are you sure?"

"Yes. Hampi is a small place. If you walk to the end of this street you'll have seen the whole town for yourself, and there's no business here of that name. And besides, alcohol is banned in Hampi, so we have no breweries. Maybe you can look up the road in Hospet."

"What about a guy called Max? Have you heard of him?"

The man gave a blank look. "No. I know most of the people in this town, but I've never heard of him."

Dig sighed. "Okay."

The man smiled. "Maybe you need to bribe an official. That's the Indian way of doing things!" He laughed. "Now, do you want to go on a tour of the ruins while you're here?"

"No thanks. Maybe later."

"A boat trip?"

"No."

"Bike tour?"

Dig shook his head.

Hari leaned in close to Dig and whispered. "Do you want a bet on the cricket? I can give you three to one on the Sunrisers tonight. You can't get a bet anywhere else in Hampi, as sports betting's illegal in Karnartaka. I'm only offering this to you as you seem like a man who likes his sport."

"No thanks. I need to hang on to all the cash I've got at the moment."

"I can get you Karcha, special rice spirit, also banned."

"Not right now."

"Hostel?"

"No, not interested," Dig said with a smile. "I tell you what though, because you've helped me, if I ever *do* need anything I'll make sure that I buy it here, okay?" He stood and made his way to the door.

"Bus ticket? Train ticket?" Hari followed him out of the building and onto the street. "Okay sir! You make sure you come back to me when you buy your tickets. For anything!" Dig gave a thumbs up, then walked up the street with Hari's voice trailing behind him.

The Hampi Bazaar was the town's main road, and Dig walked the five-hundred-metre length of it from start to finish. On the journey, he stopped in two restaurants, three hostels and a fruit stall, asking the inhabitants similar questions about the Banyan Brewery or anyone called Max. All the responses were the same, blank looks, shaking heads, or shrugged shoulders.

His concentration was evaporating in the heat, so Dig sat on a stone wall outside the temple and took a gulp of water from his bottle.

Where is it? he thought. *It can't be far away. Dad's been paying into bank accounts here for years.*

He narrowed his eyes, then removed the invoice from his pocket, this time focusing on a section at the bottom:

Preferred Payment Method: Direct Bank Transfer
Bank: Canara Bank, Hampi
Account: 0154563
IFSC Code: CNRB0001187

Back down the road, a battered fluorescent sign hung over the street. He could just make out the lettering as *Canara Bank.*

Dig pulled himself to his feet and headed toward it. A small restaurant stood opposite, so he took a seat, ordered a fruit juice, and had a closer look.

It was a formal building, with two large stone columns framing the door, and policemen in khaki uniforms flanking the entrance. One was at least six feet tall, while the other was shorter and wider. Both slung rifles over their shoulders. A steady stream of tourists and locals moved between them through the doors.

Hari's words rung in his ears. *Maybe you need to bribe an official. That's the Indian way of doing things!*

He checked his wallet and removed a thousand rupee note, folded it into a tight square and placed it in the top pocket of his shirt—his backup plan. He finished his drink, took a deep breath, and headed across the road.

The policemen were engrossed in conversation as he approached. The taller man leaned against the door jamb and gesticulated with his hands; the smaller man nodded, his fingers drumming the butt of his gun. Dig tried to enter with a relaxed, casual air about him—but instead felt like an underage kid trying to blag his way into a nightclub. Nonetheless, as he entered the taller policeman took a sideways glance and continued his conversation without breaking sentence.

Walls of stained wood panelling framed an open room with ceiling fans that spun slow revolutions. The buzz of ringing phones and murmured conversations filled the room, and the scent of toner was in the air.

Bank tellers stood behind glass on one side of the room, serving a line of customers cordoned off by guide ropes. On the other side, a man sat behind a desk with a sign announcing that he was the *Customer Enquiry* section of the bank.

Dig made his way to a rack of forms by the wall and found one entitled *Deposit Slip*. He pulled the brewery invoice from his pocket and copied the bank account numbers into the appropriate boxes.

Dig checked the note was still inside his pocket. His stomach churned; he'd never attempted to bribe someone before. Did you just hand the money straight over? Leave it on the desk? Drop it on the floor? Put it in an envelope? Was he supposed to use some kind of code word?

He glanced across at Mr Customer Service. He looked to be in his fifties. Three pens were perched neatly on the front pocket of his shirt. He supported a thick beard, and broken blood vessels tracked across his nose. A faded plastic sign on the desk read *Kumar Rangkot.*

Dig took a deep breath, grabbed the deposit slip, and crossed the room.

"Hi." Dig forced a smile. "How are you?"

Kumar gave a small nod.

"Hot out there today huh?"

Kumar raised an eyebrow. "How can I help?"

Dig took a seat. "Well, I've a small issue. I've just travelled over from Australia for a meeting with my business partner in Hampi. You see?" Dig placed the Banyan Brewery invoice on the desk between them. "And well, it looks like the jetlag's taken its toll as I've managed to misplace the address of the company." He rolled his eyes. "So I know the company's got an account with your bank as I've been sending them money here for years, but I'd appreciate if you could remind me of their address so I can make the meeting today." Dig smiled. "Here, I've filled out a slip with the account details, so if you could just write the address on here it'd be great."

Kumar glanced at the slip. "I can't give out the address of the account holder sir. If you want to transfer money to the account we can process it at the counter, but an address can't be given out."

Dig leaned closer. "Are you sure? I'm a little desperate here. I'd be very grateful if you could."

"We don't have that information sir." Kumar turned his attention to the computer screen.

Dig dropped his voice. "Look, I'll be honest with you. I really need to find that address. I've travelled a long way to get here, and if I miss this meeting then the owner, Max, will be very upset. Can you help me out? You'd be doing a favour to one of your customers."

"I don't have that information sir."

Dig had exhausted all his powers of friendly persuasion. It was time to get the big guns out. He glanced back to the entrance; the shadows of the policemen were still visible at the door.

He extracted the note from his pocket. "Okay," he whispered. "I realise that in India sometimes you have to help *grease the wheels* to make things happen. I've a thousand rupees I might accidentally drop under the desk if you help me out—know what I mean?" He winked.

The hint of a smile crept into the corners of Kumar's eyes, and he nodded. "Yes, I think I understand."

"Excellent."

"You're going to bribe me."

Dig leaned in again. "Well, if you want to put it bluntly, then yes."

Kumar stood and turned to the front door. "Officers!"

The customers in the queue turned. The taller policeman stuck his head through the front door, gun in hand.

"Arrest this man!"

Dig sat up rigid in his seat, "No!" he whispered, "I didn't mean...well...I was just joking!" A teller leant over the counter to stare, his mouth open. The two policemen pushed through the door.

Kumar stood behind his desk, hands on his hips. His eyes were wide in a manic grin. He seemed to have found some job satisfaction at Dig's expense, standing smug with the pens lined up on his creased shirt.

Dig caught his breath and blinked rapidly as a thought dawned on him. He realised he had already seen Kumar this morning—across the road at *Helpful Hari's Tourist Information*, whispering and handing over money.

The rumble of footsteps echoed across the floor as the policemen rushed through the room. Dig leaned toward Kumar. "Send them away or I'll tell them about your sports gambling."

A furrow lined Kumar's brow. "I don't know what you're talking about," he hissed, feigning an incredulous look—but Dig saw he'd touched on something.

"I saw you, this morning at the tourist office, making a bet. I reckon if the police emptied your pockets, they'd find a slip for tonight's cricket match."

Kumar frowned as the footfalls grew closer.

"Tell me the brewery address and I'll keep quiet." Dig pushed the deposit slip across the desk, then a grip clutched at his wrist, twisting it roughly behind his back, tearing a needle of pain through his shoulder.

"What's going on?" said a voice in Dig's ear.

Kumar's eyes narrowed and he folded his arms.

"What is it?" the policeman repeated. "What did he do?"

The room stood quiet, save for the slow revolution of the fan above their heads.

"Kumar?"

"Let him go," Kumar said. "I made a mistake. I misheard something he said."

"Are you sure?"

"Yes, yes, my fault." Kumar turned to the room. "I'm sorry everyone, back to work please." He retrieved the deposit slip from the desk, carefully selected a blue pen from his top pocket, and scrawled onto the paper.

The policemen frowned, and the grip on Dig's arm loosened. Dig rubbed at his elbow.

"But I'd like this man to leave. And take his forms away with him." He jammed the deposit slip into the front pocket of Dig's shirt, then refolded his arms across his chest with eyes like pinpricks.

The policeman pushed Dig sideways. "Okay, I'm going." Dig shrugged him away and headed to the exit; customers frowned as they watched him leave. When he reached the door someone shoved him between his shoulder blades.

Dig exited the bank and paced down the road, ducking through street stalls as he rotated his shoulder, trying to work away the pain. When he reached the temple at the end of the street, he sat on the warm gravel of the road with his back against the wall, and retrieved the crumpled wad of paper from his pocket.

I got it, he thought, and smiled.

He flattened the paper out between his legs. A message had been scribbled onto it in a messy blue scrawl:

I told you - there is no address on file you idiot!

Dig stared at the paper, eyes wide, then turned it over. He found nothing written on the opposite side, so he turned it back and reread it.

Dig's hands fell to his lap, and his head dropped back to the wall behind him. He stared up at the sky and sighed.

Now what?

8

HE SAT AGAINST THE WALL with the sun bearing down on him, roasting his arms and legs. Somewhere in the temple behind him a bell resonated periodically in a deep tone. As his throat parched with thirst, he threw his pack onto his back, and trudged back up the road.

When he came upon the doors of *Helpful Hari's Tourist Information* he paused, then pushed through the curtain of beads over the doorway. Hari waited inside with a smile.

"Mr Australia!" he said. "Shane Warne! David Warner! What can I help you with?"

Dig smiled weakly and pointed to a sign hanging above a bank of dusty desktop computers. A stout boy wearing headphones sat before one of the screens, playing computer games. "It says here that you arrange international phone calls?"

"Of course. Would you like to ring Australia?"

"Yes please."

"Okay, sit down." He gestured to a glass booth in the corner of the room with a telephone bolted to the wall and a green plastic stool in the centre of the space.

Dig entered the booth and pulled the sliding glass door behind him with a creak. He sat on the stool and Hari pointed at the telephone, holding his fist to his ear with thumb and pinkie finger extended.

Dig gave a thumbs up, then lifted the telephone and dialled. It rang a few times, before being picked up with a melody of tones.

"Buckley's Brewery."

"Jake, it's Dig."

"Oh, hey," Jake said. "How's it going? You get there okay?"

"Yep, I'm here. Just arrived in Hampi." The line crackled. "Got a favour to ask though...I need you to cancel my phone. It got nicked."

"How'd you manage that?"

"Taxi driver I think."

"You numpty. Yeah I'll get it stopped."

"Thanks." He swapped the phone to his other ear. "So...how are things over there?"

"I'm catching up on things. I got into Dad's computer and I'm filling last week's orders."

"Nice."

"Yeah it's amazing what I can get through without a hangover." He snorted. "So when are you planning on seeing our...friends?"

"Soon. Once I find them. I'm having a bit of trouble tracking them down. Either nobody knows where they are, or nobody wants to tell me. I'm not sure which it is at the moment."

"Bugger."

"Can you check something else for me though? Just before I left I was looking through Dad's stuff, and I remember seeing an email between him and Banyan Breweries, just before he went over to India last time."

"Last year?"

"Yeah. There was something in it about a meeting point."

"Hang on, I'll check." The squeal of the office chair echoed in the background. "Man," Jake muttered. "I don't think Dad deleted anything in here his whole life." There was a long pause. "Hang on, this might be it. Want me to read it out?"

"Yeah."

"So Dad writes: *Hi Max, I expect to arrive in Hampi mid-morning Thursday. Are you going to be around? Shaun.* And then he gets a reply: *I'll be here. If you go to the usual spot by the old train line we'll pick you up. Max.*"

"Yeah that's the one."

"Any use?"

Dig sighed. "Well it's better than nothing." The line crackled and hissed.

"Look, if things are too hard over there—"

"No, it's fine," Dig said in a strained voice.

"Don't be afraid to come home okay?"

"Yeah, I may have to at this rate."

They said goodbye, and Dig replaced the phone in its cradle. He stared at it for a moment, then pushed open the door of the booth.

Hari looked up. "Finished?"

Dig nodded, and walked to the counter. From across the room, the boy's computer screen echoed with the sound of canned gunshot.

Hari nodded toward the boy. "My nephew," he said. "All he does is play *Call of Duty*." He shook his head. "So how was mummy then?"

Dig smiled. "My brother actually, and he's fine." Below him, a map was spread beneath the glass of the counter. "What do you know about old railway lines in Hampi?"

"As in not used?"

"Yeah, I think so."

"Well the old Anjaneya line closed down years ago. But it's still in there somewhere, covered in weeds."

"It is close to here?"

Hari pointed to the map. "It runs from the back of town and heads north around the heritage area. But nobody goes there. You'd see better sights on the main trails. Would you like to rent a trail bike?"

"I've never ridden a motorbike before."

"Don't worry, it's easy to figure out. I'll show you."

Dig shrugged. "Okay. And I'll take a map."

"Excellent."

Hari ducked into a doorway and reappeared with a dusty yellow trail bike. He pushed it through the shop and out into the street. Dig followed him.

They stood together on the road shoulder, behind the line of street stalls. Dig shielded his eyes from the sun as Hari gestured to the bike. "Okay," he said. "Sit down."

Dig swung his leg over the machine and balanced stiffly on the seat.

"Right," Hari said. "Left hand lever's the clutch, right hand grip's the throttle, right hand lever is front brake, right foot is the rear brake and left foot is to change gears. Understand?"

Dig frowned and looked at the controls. "I think so."

"Oh, and as you move up through the gears it goes gear one, then neutral, then two, three and four."

"Why does it do that?"

Hari looked at him blankly. "I don't know. I'm a travel agent, not a mechanic! Now put the clutch in and start it up."

Dig squeezed the lever on his left hand and turned a key on the dash. The motor roared into life, vibrating between Dig's legs.

"Now let out the clutch and give it some throttle!"

Dig frowned, then winced as he twisted back the throttle on his right hand and let out the clutch on his left. The engine whined and jerked forward, then puttered out to a stall.

Hari shook his head. "Try again. But slower."

Dig pursed his lips, then squeezed the clutch and started the machine back up. He took a breath, eased on the throttle, and slowly let out the clutch. The bike jumped forward and cruised along the dirt.

"Good!" Hari shouted. "Now change gears!"

Dig glanced backwards, eyes wide. "How do I do that again?"

"Your feet!"

Dig studied his feet as he wavered along the road. He spotted a lever by his toes and pushed it down; the engine screamed while the bike lost power. He pressed it again and the bike shot forward, rocking Dig's head back, the front wheel lifting off the ground.

As the wheel returned to the dirt the bike jerked to the right, directly at a market stall full of clothes. Dig tried to wrestle the handlebars straight again, but it was too late, and he punched into the rear of the stall. The hanging shirts wrapped around his head, tipping the bike backwards. He hit the ground heavily, and the handlebars bounced off his chest before clattering to the ground beside him. A muffled gaggle of voices approached, and the shirts were pulled from his face to reveal Hari standing over him.

"Are you okay?"

Dig clutched at his chest and grimaced. "I think so," he said. "Just fell pretty hard."

"Up then." Hari held out a hand. Dig grasped it and was pulled to his feet.

"He's very sorry," Hari said to the shopkeeper and placed his palms together at his chest. He pulled the bike upright and wheeled it back toward his shop, gesturing for Dig to follow.

"Sorry," Dig repeated to the stall owner, and hobbled after him.

Hari leaned the motorbike against the shopfront. "Wait here," he said. "I've just the thing." He disappeared through the doorway.

Dig knelt forward on the dirt, panting and rubbing at his chest. Hari reappeared through the curtain of beads, pushing a rusted pink pushbike. It had curved handlebars, yellow streamers dangling from the handles, and a bent wicker basket hanging from the front. The wheels were large and the tyres thin.

"Your new ride!" Hari said.

Dig frowned.

9

A HOT WIND BLEW THROUGH Dig's hair as he weaved his new pushbike between pedestrians on the Hampi bazaar. His daypack was hooked across his shoulders and a one page tourist map jammed into his back pocket. Dogs barked at his ankles as he pedalled.

He followed the road until the street stalls and restaurants dropped away, leaving a wide dirt path that thinned out and tracked past a sign that announced the start of the natural heritage area. Dig eased the bike to a halt beside the sign.

Ahead, a wide expanse of triangular hills stood before a hazy blue sky. Piles of beige, sun bleached boulders were spread across the hills with small stone buildings nestled amongst them. A carpet of tropical green palms circled their base. It was an imposing landscape that seemed like a sandpit for the children of giants.

The dirt road continued past the sign and snaked into the distance between the hills. Dig checked his map, then pushed his bike into motion and pedalled away down the road.

He followed the path across a rocky field before Dig spotted what he was looking for—twin sections of rusted steel running perpendicular to the path, nearly buried in the ground. It was a crossing over the old railway line.

Dig parked his bike and surveyed the horizon. Birds chirped in the distance and a light breeze blew clouds of dust up at his feet, but otherwise all was still. No modern buildings could be seen, and certainly nothing that resembled a brewery.

What am I doing? he thought. *This can't be the right place. Why would Dad ever come out here?*

On each side of the crossing, the path of the old rail line carved a cutting through the rocky landscape. Dark timber sleepers were partially visible below the tracks, amongst an overgrowth of pointed brown grass and spiky weeds.

Dig glanced toward Hampi, then rolled the front wheel of the bike to sit between the parallel railway tracks heading north. He placed his foot on the pedal and pushed the bike forward.

The bike had no shocks and the padding on the seat was sparse. As the wheels rumbled along the timber sleepers Dig felt every bump and groove reverberate through the frame. He sat forward and concentrated on the ground ahead as he dodged the weeds between the tracks. Periodically the rims would bottom out, sending a shockwave through the bicycle frame and directly into his rear end.

He followed the rails around the base of a wide hill where tall grass whipped at his shins. The track veered downhill into a cluster of dense tropical palms crowding tightly on both sides of the track. Overhanging vines pulled at his face.

The palms opened out to reveal a wide river, and he followed the tracks over a weathered timber bridge. The water below the bridge was dark, and flowed slowly, with large leaves travelling on the surface. Long reeds grew on the banks.

The track then began to rise, and Dig stood up to pump the pedals harder. His thighs burned as his breathing increased.

A large hill crested the horizon. The landscape around him became rockier, and piles of boulders rose up beside the rails. The track curved around a bend and headed directly toward the dark semi-circle of a tunnel; the rails disappeared into the hole.

Dig let the bike cruise to a standstill at the opening. He was breathing heavily, and he fished his water bottle from his pack to gulp down a few mouthfuls.

Cylindrical rock columns flanked either side of the tunnel, and a stone arch spanned across the top with a series of unfamiliar characters carved into it. A small bird with blue and green feathers was perched on top of the arch. Its head was buried under one wing, preening itself.

He stepped off the bike and propped it against the rocky cutting beside the track, then approached the darkness. He moved cautiously, feeling like an unwelcome visitor to an ancient home. As he reached the opening, he eased his head inside and waited for his eyes to adjust to the gloom.

It was damp and cool, and the hairs on the back of Dig's neck crept to attention. The rail line continued on, curving slowly into the depths of the hill. Black streaks of ash ran down the walls. Water dripped from the ceiling and formed stagnant pools beside the rails.

Dig stepped into the tunnel. His foot sunk into a fine, mushy silt between the tracks; it smelled dank and peaty, of damp earth and stale smoke. Claustrophobia crept up on him, but his curiosity compelled him forward.

As he stepped further inside he became increasingly aware of a deep resonant hum, like an electrical substation. He froze and listened, trying to fathom what kind of thing could create such a sound.

He stared into the darkness, and thought he saw something moving at the edge of his vision, like a dark swirling mass. A flutter danced in his chest and he rubbed at his eyes. Something wasn't right about this place. It was time to leave.

He turned and strode back toward the entrance—then before he realised it—he was running, his feet splashing through the mushy silt and throwing mud up into the air.

His big toe slammed into something hard and pointed, likely some type of fixing for the rail line. He pitched forward and fell to his side, just inside the tunnel opening. Cold liquid seeped into the fabric of his shorts.

"Crap!" he muttered, and as he pushed to his feet he heard a familiar buzzing sound ahead of him. He looked up and froze.

Sunlight illuminated the arch of the doorway, and a small shape flew through the opening at head height. It moved toward Dig and then stopped, zipping from side to side in the air. Dig's heart skipped when he realised what it was—a wasp.

And further, this wasn't just an ordinary wasp. It was some kind of monster, double the size of any wasp he'd ever seen—and as long and thick as his thumb. Its orange head framed two deep black crescents for eyes. At its jawline, two serrated, scissor-like mandibles slowly opened and closed, as if picking up his scent. Its upper body was dark furry brown with a tint of gold, and a black stinger protruded from its rear like the point of a needle. The stinger pulsated in and out, as if itching to strike.

Dig clenched his teeth. He contemplated running, but the creature hung in the air ahead of him, blocking his path. Instead, he remained still and willed it to lose interest and fly away.

But somehow, Dig knew it wouldn't. It was something about the way the wasp whipped back and forth through the air, as if taunting him, wanting him to flee. It projected a menacing presence that only knew one method of operation—attack.

Its wings buzzed with increased intensity and it flew at him.

Dig swiped at it and missed—but he disturbed enough air to send it off course, and the wasp zipped past his ear, then circled around and returned to its previous position above his head. He pushed up from the ground with one hand, and held the other protectively in front of him.

The sunlight at the tunnel entrance suddenly broke, and a second shadow cruised toward him, high above his head, then dove down, directly at him. Dig cowered and squinted, and made out the shape of a two wide wings and a beak.

It was a bird—the same bird he had seen perched on the top of tunnel arch. Its green and blue wings were spread in a wide glide, and its head was tucked in.

The bird swooped and plucked the wasp from the air, then eased upwards, flapped twice, and dropped to the floor, coming to a rest on one of the steel tracks.

The wasp writhed in its beak, its stinger reaching out for a strike, but the bird bent down and hammered the creature against the rail until it stopped moving. It dropped the insect into its throat, tilted its head to study Dig for moment, and launched back out of the tunnel with a flap of wings. Dig tried to regain his breath.

A new rumbling echoed down the passage. Dig frowned as the tunnel filled with light and a bright white headlight tracked around the bend. His heart skipped a beat.

A train? Dig thought. *Is that possible?*

The rumble grew louder as the machine approached, reverberating off the tunnel walls. Small rocks dropped from the ceiling, splashing into the pools of water beside the tracks. The headlight grew brighter, and Dig squinted as the walls of the passage were lit with an eerie clarity. He considered running, but the machine was already too close. Instead, he leapt sideways off the track and dropped to the ground.

His shoulder hit the sodden earth and liquid splashed into his ear. He wrapped his arms around his head, bracing for impact.

There was a squeal of brakes and a hitching, skidding sound, before he was covered in a shower of gravel. The noise dropped to a low reverberation.

After a moment, Dig dared to open his eyes. Beside him, the figure of a young boy sat on a motorbike.

"Are you okay?" the boy said. "You took a tumble there."

Dig took deep breaths, trying to restrain the pace of his heart. "Oh man..." he said. "You scared the shit out of me. I thought you were...a train."

The boy frowned. "Sorry. But you *were* sitting in the middle of the tracks. Not smart."

Dig pursed his lips. "I was...being harassed by a monster wasp."

"A hornet you mean."

"Huh?"

"Asian giant hornets. Like wasps, but much bigger and meaner. There's a nest inside this tunnel."

Dig thought back to the humming resonance he had heard. It made sense. He nodded.

"Those things aren't friendly," the boy said.

"I noticed."

"You should get out of here."

"Don't mind if I do." Dig laboured to his feet. He wiped the mud from his palms to his thighs, then shuffled back out through the tunnel entrance to the sunlight. He stepped down the track embankment, and stood with his back against the rock wall. He could taste mud on his lips, and he wiped it away with the back of his hand.

The boy followed him out of the tunnel and cruised the motorbike to a stop beside him. He had cropped brown hair and looked to be around twelve years old. "What are you doing here anyway?"

Dig considered his answer, thinking back to Jake's words about his father's email. "I'm here for a...meeting," he lied.

"With who?"

"With...Max."

The boy's back straightened and he lifted his chin. "Does Max know about this?"

"Yes...Max just told me to wait here and someone would pick me up."

"Nobody said anything to me."

Dig shrugged. "Should I just keeping waiting then?"

The boy scratched at the side of his face. "Nobody tells me anything," he muttered, and sighed. "I suppose I can take you over."

"Thanks."

The boy turned the bike around and faced back into the tunnel. "Okay, you better hop on."

Dig stared at the black opening and swallowed. "What about the hornets?"

"If we ride fast enough, they won't get us."

"And what if you have to stop?"

"We won't stop. If we stop, the hornets will sting us to death—so we won't stop."

Dig's brow furrowed. "I'm allergic to wasps."

"Ha! Well you really don't want to get stung then."

"Promise we won't?"

"You won't if you do what I tell you."

Dig raised his eyebrows, then climbed onto the back of the bike.

The boy extended his hand backwards. "I'm Raj."

"Dig."

"Are you Australian?"

"Yep."

"Aah. Shane Warne and Michael Clarke. Good cricketers."

"They are," Dig said with a weak smile.

"Now, tuck in any loose folds of clothing—like your shorts. You don't want to pick up any hitchhikers on the way through. And keep your head down. Right?" Dig nodded and took hold of the frame of the bike behind his rear.

Raj revved the engine twice before kicking it into gear with a lurch. The wheel skidded and threw up mud behind them, before finding purchase and setting off.

They followed the rails into the tunnel at a pace that felt like it was two gears faster than was required. The cool air whipped at Dig's eyes and made them water; he gripped the frame of the bike so tightly his knuckles ached. He peeked over the top of Raj's shoulder.

The headlight threw out a wall of light that travelled a short space ahead of them. The rail continued to bend away into the hill, flanked on either side by ragged walls hammered directly through the bedrock. Light reflected off rivulets that tracked down the stone. The engine echoed loudly.

The path of the tunnel straightened, and Dig ducked away from a few solitary hornets that zipped toward him.

The track swung to the left and the bike rumbled below Dig's rear. The density of hornets increased until they filled the path of the headlight like a thick, swirling sandstorm. Dig's shoulders tensed and his heart raced.

A rectangular timber box hung in the top corner of the tunnel, housing a dusty signal light. Nestled beside it was a fibrous, multi-layered chandelier. It was the wasp nest, and a mass of hornets buzzed around it in a dense fog.

The bike raced toward the cloud of insects and Raj leaned forward and dropped his head. Dig did the same, tucking his chin into his chest and bracing for impact.

As they plunged into the swarm, wasps hammered into their heads and shoulders with a sickening patter. The bodies of the creatures burst apart under the impact, spewing a shower of liquid hornet internals across Dig's face. Tiny wings fluttered past his ears. He wanted to scream but he dared not open his mouth, so the sound caught in his throat in a guttural moan.

Eventually, the splattering gave way to the reverberation of the engine around the walls—then they burst into fresh air. Sunlight warmed the back of Dig's neck. They were outside again, and he allowed himself to breathe, before wiping madly at his face and hair with one hand as they bounced along the tracks. He opened his eyes to see the ground rushing past below them. Then as he lifted his gaze, he broke into a grin.

The rail line had exited the tunnel along a ridge that tracked down a steep valley. In the base of the valley was a long, flat meadow. Spread across the meadow, in an area that covered more than ten football fields, were rows upon rows of leafy green vines that climbed two stories into the air, growing up an ordered grid of timber poles and interconnecting wires.

Dig shook his head slowly. He leant forward to Raj and shouted. "Those are hop vines?"

Raj nodded, the wind blowing the hair back from his face. "The brewery's down by the river," he said. "I'll take you there."

Dig looked over Raj's shoulder; his gaze followed the path of the rail as it cut a straight line down the ridge toward a wide, brown river. As the tracks reached the shore, the rail rose up into the air and stopped abruptly at the naked timber pylons of a washed out bridge.

Two buildings stood on the river bank: a tall building with a corrugated roof and white smoke wafting out of a chimney, and a small residential shack, nestled amongst the trees.

Dig took a deep breath and nodded to himself as the wind whistled in his ears. He had finally found the Banyan Brewery. How many times had his father ridden down this same path during his life?

But, now he was here, he needed to concentrate on what lay ahead. He'd arrived unannounced into one of the most remote areas of India, and was about to meet a group who had demonstrated a troubling level of casual brutality. His stomach churned as he recalled Jake's hand, and the ripping tear as the knife carved through the finger. He remembered Jake screaming. The fear. The panic. And Shiv's words:

I'm looking at two hopheads who seem incapable of taking care of themselves, let alone become competent business partners.

He glanced at his clothes. His shorts and shirt were covered in mud. His body was sweat soaked and greasy. His face was covered in insect internals. He didn't want to ruin a first impression for the second time.

Dig bit his lip, then leaned forward to Raj, shouting over the noise of the engine. "Is there somewhere I can quickly wash up and change my clothes before I go into the brewery?"

Raj's brow furrowed. "There's a shower in the house. Want me to take you there first?"

"Yeah, that would be good."

Raj nodded, and steered the bike down the ridge. At the bottom, he turned it off the tracks and flanked the edge of the hop fields toward the house. Dig recognised the familiar orange tinge on the flowers as they passed.

The house was constructed of pale yellow brick and brown tile, and surrounded by a wide concrete veranda before a patch of brown, untended grass. A thicket of squat brown trees crowded behind the house, and a flock of chirping white birds flew out from them as they arrived. The front door stood open.

Raj rolled the bike to a stop outside, then switched off the engine. "Come on." He walked inside.

Dig followed, ducking through a low doorway into an open-plan kitchen and lounge. Stools were set up by a granite kitchen bench, and a spicy, milky fragrance filled the air. On the far wall, a sliding glass door opened onto a deck that flanked the shoulder of the river—a wide brown expanse of slow moving water.

Raj squatted by a cupboard in the corner of the room, then held a towel out to Dig. "Here," he said. "The shower's through that door." He pointed to a bi-fold door beside the deck.

"Thanks." Dig took the towel through to a small room of rendered cement. He washed himself down, changed into a new T-shirt and shorts, and surveyed himself. While he didn't feel like a high-powered executive, he certainly felt more equipped to handle a business negotiation that had the prosperity of his family riding on it.

He returned to the main room with the wet towel hanging limply in his hand. Raj sat at a chair by the kitchen counter, nursing a glass cup. A jug of milky liquid sat on the counter beside him.

"Chai?" Raj said.

Dig looked at him blankly.

"Chai," Raj repeated. "Tea."

"Oh right, sure."

Raj poured a second helping from the jug and placed the cup on the table before Dig. He held up his own glass and beckoned for Dig to do the same. Dig lifted the cup to his lips and took a sip. It was milky, sweet and tasted of cinnamon. "Wow."

"You like it?"

"Yeah, it's great." Dig's attention caught on a framed picture on the wall beside him. It depicted three people in a family pose: a middle-aged man with a thick beard and a confused expression; a short, stocky woman with hair tied back in a bun; and Raj sitting between them, hands folded on his lap.

"Your parents?"

Raj nodded.

On the wall beside it was a second framed picture, showing two men standing formally on a stage. Dig recognised Raj's father. He wore an academic robe, and stood stiffly with startled eyes and a pasted-on smile as he was handed a decorative piece of paper. A heading inscribed below the picture read: *Girish Survana – Doctorate in Botany – Delhi University.*

"A botanist huh?"

Raj glanced at the picture. "Yes, Dad and I manage the crops around here."

"Impressive. Our company uses your hops to make our beer. We think they could be the best in the world."

Raj lowered his glass to the table and studied Dig, his eyebrows furrowed. "You're lucky," he said. "We don't export many hops. Most are kept for our own production."

"But how do you get the hops out of here?"

"Same way you came in."

"What, by motorbike?"

"By rail. Deliveries leave most evenings."

"But—I didn't see any trains?"

"Don't need them," said Raj, smiling. "Now stop asking questions and I'll drop you over for your meeting." He beckoned Dig to the door.

They remounted the motorbike, and Raj steered it through a pair of deep wheel ruts that traced the edge of the river. They bounced through potholes as the imposing frame of the brewery grew closer. Dig clenched his teeth and held tightly to the frame of the bike.

10

RAJ EASED THE BIKE TO A STOP in a dirt car park outside the rusted, corrugated building. A cluster of motorbikes were lined up on one side of the clearing; a long container truck was parked opposite. Flanking the edge of the river were a cluster of squat trees with branches that stretched wide over the dirt, and roots that hung down in curtains. Dig recognised the banyan trees from the invoice in his pocket.

He followed Raj toward a wide, open roller door that revealed the shadowy interior of the brewery. As he passed the container truck he spotted a set of circular steel railway wheels on the machine that were set forward of the normal rubber tyres.

"The truck also has rail wheels?"

"It's a hi-rail," Raj said. "It travels on both."

Dig raised his eyebrows and nodded.

A dented orange forklift drove out of the building, supporting a pallet of green boxes with *Banyan Bitter* marked on the side, and headed to the rear of the container truck. As the machine lowered the pallet into the container, the thick-bearded driver watched Dig with narrowed eyes. Dig took a deep breath and followed Raj through the door.

The inside of the building opened out to a high ceiling of exposed steel rafters. A pair of pigeons took flight above them; the flapping of their wings echoed around the space.

At ground level, a boxy office building of peeling green paint was set against the near wall. Further inside, hissing pieces of rusted brewing equipment were clustered together in groups. A sulphuric odour hung in the air.

Dig followed Raj around the corner of the office to see a group of three men standing over a weathered steel vat. One was elderly with hunched shoulders, wild grey hair and a thick beard. He wore only a length of fabric tied around his waist. The other men poured bags of grain into the vat, their hair spotted with barley husk. Raj walked past them and headed toward the office, with Dig behind him.

"Hey!" said a high pitched voice. Dig turned to see the elderly man staring at him as he scratched his face. "Who...is this?" Dig recognised him as Raj's father, Girish, from the pictures inside the house.

"His name's Dig," Raj said. "I'm taking him in for a meeting with Max."

Girish blinked rapidly. "What? Um...no Raj! Max is out at the docks today, in the Goa office." He continued to scratch at his face. "But, who *is* this?"

An awkward silence filled the room. Nausea churned in Dig's stomach as he stepped forward and extended a hand. "Hi, I'm Dig."

"Stop." Girish folded his arms. "What are you doing here?"

"Please. I apologise for turning up unannounced, but I need to have a quick talk to Max. Or if he isn't here, then maybe *we* can have a quick chat."

Girish's brow furrowed. "No, no. I don't do...*chats*. I don't think you understand what you have..." His voice trailed away. "How did you find this place?"

Dig glanced toward Raj. "My father was a business associate of Max. But things have changed, and I need to discuss something with him."

Girish's face blotched red and sweat beaded across his forehead. "Max isn't here, and won't be for days." He turned to Raj. "Did you bring him in here?"

Raj stood stiffly. "He said he had a meeting."

"And so you just drove him in here?"

Raj's gaze dropped to the floor.

"Oh my..." Girish pulled at his ear and paced in front of the vat. "Max is going to...well...be upset."

Dig eyed the path back toward the door. "Is there anyone else I can talk to?"

"No!" Girish said. "There is *nobody* to talk to. You shouldn't be here. You're a very silly boy."

Dig glanced around at the room. "Well maybe if you can tell me where Max is, I'll head over there instead."

"Ha!" Girish snorted. "Oh no. You won't be leaving now. You've dug your own grave in that regard."

An emptiness balled in the pit of Dig's stomach. "Hang on," he said. "There's no need for that." He took a step backward, and the two men beside Girish dropped their sacks of grain to the ground.

Girish paced again and shook his head. He turned to Raj. "You see what you did? If you drop your guard you create needless suffering."

Dig took another step backward, and Raj appeared at his shoulder to grab his arm. Dig tried to pull it away, but Raj held tight.

"Hey Raj," Dig said. "Let go mate."

Raj lifted his chin. "You lied to me."

"I had to bud." Dig lifted his foot. "And sorry, but I also have to do this." He brought his foot down hard on Raj's toes. Raj grunted and Dig pulled his arm free, then turned and ran for the exit.

"Get him," Girish shouted in a high pitched squeal. A scurry of feet followed him toward the door.

Dig pumped his arms and ran as fast as he could, skidding around the corner of the office, before he straightened and headed for the opening. Voices shouted behind him.

He burst into the sunlight and skidded to a stop in the dirt. To his left, the path led away up the ridge. To his right, the cluster of motorbikes sat together beside the banyan trees.

Dig swore, then darted across the patch of dirt toward the trees. He found Raj's motorbike in the collection of machines and sat down.

He stared at the controls for a moment before he depressed the clutch and turned a small key on the instrument panel. The bike hummed into life. He frantically turned the bike around and faced it into the carpark. To his left, Raj and the two men ran through the door of the brewery, shouting.

Dig took a breath, then revved the engine and dropped the clutch. The bike jerked forward, fishtailing wide arcs left and right in the dirt. He struggled to control it.

One of the men ran ahead of him and tried to block his path out of the carpark. Dig wrenched the handlebars to the right, but the man lunged and hooked a handful of his backpack. The motorbike veered sideways, and Dig fought to keep it upright before the man's grip broke. The bike shot forward, wavering between potholes in the dirt.

The engine roared, and Dig began stamping at the gear lever. The bike jerked and spluttered, but he held tightly to the handlebars and kept it pointed forward.

He dared a glance behind him: the group of men gesticulated as they dragged a second motorbike into the middle of the car park. Dig ducked into the headwind and pulled the throttle back as far as it would allow, gripping it so tightly that his knuckles turned white.

He followed the rutted dirt track past the house, and then up the small rise to the old railway line. He directed the front wheel between the tracks and bounced through tufts of grass as the bike climbed the ridge.

The wind bit at his eyes and whistled in his ears as he sped up the track. He concentrated on the four foot of space between the two lengths of rusted steel below him, the looming wall of rock ahead, and the black crescent of tunnel that approached. He hunched his shoulders, ducked his head and pointed the handlebars into the shadows.

The darkness enveloped him; he frantically pawed at the dashboard and flicked random levers, searching for a headlight. The flickering strobe of an indicator blinked twice before the headlights burst to life, illuminating a tight passage of water soaked stone. The echo of the engine reverberated off the walls.

Ahead, he could see the first signs of the hornets circulating in the air, and he glanced down at his exposed arms and hands. His grip on the throttle loosened; the engine dropped in revs as he considered stopping.

But instead, he ducked low in his seat, tipped his forehead down, gritted his teeth, and whipped the throttle back to full.

The first hornet bounced off the top of his ear with a buzzing hum, and he flinched away. The second hit him in the bridge of the nose and exploded—splatting liquid internals into his eye. The third disintegrated high on his forehead, and he felt juice track down his temple and over his cheekbone.

Soon after, the air morphed into a writhing body of insects. He ducked his head further and closed his eyes to slits. The hornets were everywhere at once, pounding into his knuckles, across his forehead, and into his elbows and legs, a fluttering, buzzing wall of fury, breaking apart and splattering through his hair and ears, innards dripping down his nose and off the end of his chin.

Dig pressed his lips together and held his breath, blinking rapidly, trying to maintain sight of the rails ahead of him.

Then, as quick as the insects appeared, they were behind him. Dig straightened and wiped at his face, then spat—trying to rid himself of the sour taste on his lips.

The rail line swung to the left and the doorway of light appeared ahead. He gripped the throttle with a renewed sense of determination as the bike broke out into sunlight on the opposite side of the hill.

The rocky cutting dropped away, and Dig spotted his pushbike still propped neatly against the wall. He continued past it.

The ground between the tracks was bumpier here, and he dropped his speed down a couple of notches. He took a quick glance behind him, but saw no signs of his pursuers. He nodded to himself and kept his concentration on the track ahead. The rail dropped down and approached the river.

A vibration buzzed in his armpit, and his heart raced. With wide eyes, he lifted his arm to examine the loose fold of fabric hanging at his shirt sleeve. Inside the shirt sat an unwelcome passenger—a fat, writhing, hairy hornet of brown and yellow, with stinger extended.

Dig grimaced, then struck at the fabric of his shirt, trying to force the creature out. But the furry mass remained intact—now shimmering with a new intensity. It stood with its abdomen curled up, trying to sting anything it could get a purchase on.

Dig pressed his index finger behind his thumb and gave the insect a solid flick through the fabric. It shot out the sleeve opening and flew away.

Dig breathed rapidly as he turned his attention back to the track, only to see the front wheel impact hard against the rusted rail. He overcorrected and the tyre bounced up and over the opposite side.

The bike trundled down the side of the embankment, headed for a tangle of shrubbery on the edge of the river. He pulled on the brakes and the wheel slid away in the ballast before smashing hard into a bulbous rock. Dig catapulted forward over the handlebars, arms splayed.

He crashed into a tangle of spiky branches that tore at his arms and face. Something solid caught him around the waist, rotating him sideways as the air rushed out of his lungs. His shoulder slammed into the ground.

The bike fell beside him with a whining clatter. The engine spluttered and cut out, and the air filled with a sudden quiet, save for the ticking metronome of the front wheel as it spun revolutions beside his head.

Dig tried to regain his breath, but his lungs were frozen. For a terrifying moment he thought he would suffocate, but then he managed a wheezing intake, followed by a rapid series of short breaths. He could taste blood in his mouth, and rolled to his elbows and spat into the earth. His ribs screamed at him; his head rang with adrenaline; he closed his eyes and waited for the pain to subside.

He heard the whine of a motorbike, and turned to see a screen of broken shrubbery standing between him and the railway embankment. He tried to crawl away but his ribs protested.

The rev of the distant motorbike increased—and through the screen of branches he recognised the silhouette of Raj as he motored the machine along the track. Dig ducked, but the boy passed by without a glance.

The engine rumbled as it crossed the river bridge and then rose up the far bank, heading for Hampi. Eventually, the sound petered out until Dig was left with only the birds chirping in the branches above his head. He stared at the sky, taking deep breaths.

He lay there until the sun dropped low on the horizon. The clouds floated past while the frogs croaked from the river bank. He considered walking the rail line back to town, but didn't want to risk meeting Raj on a return trip. Instead, he wrapped an arm across his sore ribs, and thought about his visit to the Banyan Brewery.

He considered Raj and his father, the botanist—the man responsible for cultivating the high quality hops. He thought about the remote position of the brewery and the effort they made to export their goods.

How had his father developed a relationship with these people?

And what about Max?

Raj's father, Girish, had said Max was at the docks, organising a delivery. As they were eight hundred kilometres from the coast, the docks were a long way away.

And what about Girish's other words: *Oh no, you aren't leaving now!*

All he had seen was a normally functioning brewery, with no major difference to his family setup at home—barring the fact that it was near impossible to find.

Even worse, by turning up at the brewery unannounced, and then making an escape, had he soured any chance of salvaging the business relationship?

And was going home an option now? They knew where Dig and his family lived. Had Dig's visit triggered some new repercussion?

He didn't know, and his head ached as he thought about it. Either way, he was likely now in worse trouble than when he arrived in India.

He closed his eyes and tried to block it all out.

Sometime later, he was woken by the distant whine of a motorbike as it approached from the river. The space around him had filled with shadows—the last remnants of a sunset burned behind the hills.

The motorbike dropped down a couple of gears as it crossed the bridge, then powered up again as it climbed the bank. Dig lay down amongst the shrubs and waited for it to pass.

The bright headlight drove past him, heading for the tunnel. Dig lifted his head and again recognised the silhouette of Raj in the seat.

The whine of the engine took on a hollow quality as it entered the tunnel. Then all was silent again, save for the static of the river as it pushed past the columns of the bridge.

Dig pulled his backpack to him and gave the contents a quick check. He was surprised there seemed to be little damage. He retrieved his water bottle and took a sip, swishing it around in his mouth before he spat it out into the dirt, then took a few long drafts.

He crawled across the undergrowth to examine the motorbike. It lay on its side, twisted and broken, with the front forks bent. The seat had popped open, and the storage section had spilled out a worn pair of overalls and a cracked bike helmet. Oil dripped from the engine, covering the leaves in a thick ooze.

Dig gingerly pushed himself to his feet, favouring his injured side, and took a few steps forward. His calves were caked in dirt.

He pushed his way through the underbrush and climbed the embankment. As he stood between the tracks he studied the rails as they dropped down over the bridge, heading for Hampi.

Dig wanted to begin the walk back, to reach Hampi, find a bus back to Mumbai, and a plane back to Australia. He was already battered and bruised, and fatigue was setting in hard.

But he didn't. He had come this far, and there was too much at stake to stop now.

He examined the base of the embankment where he had crashed into the bushes. A gnarled branch lay on the ground—as thick as his arm and a few metres long. One end was freshly splintered, snapped from a nearby tree. Dig guessed it had been ripped off by the motorbike during his crash.

He shuffled down the embankment to the branch, placed a foot on each side of it, then squatted and lifted one end. It was heavy and awkward, but he managed to drag it up the side of the embankment. When he reached the crest he laid it out perpendicular to the tracks.

As he surveyed his work, he thought back to the words of Raj and Girish:

—*Max is out at the docks today, in the Goa office.*

—*deliveries leave most nights.*

He rubbed at his temples, then stepped down the embankment and pushed back into the greenery until he found the base of a solid tree. He stamped the ground down around it, creating a flat area of broken ferns and moss. He then sat down, placed his back against the tree, closed his eyes, and waited.

A loud rumble and a squeal of brakes ripped him back into consciousness. The air felt murky and cold and his arms and legs itched. He waved at a cloud of feasting bugs.

Ahead of him through the branches, two cones of light penetrated the gloom. Dig lifted himself to his feet, pulled on his pack, and crept closer to the embankment.

The hi-rail truck was parked a few metres short of the branch that blocked the tracks; its headlights threw a bright spotlight over its length. The hiss of air brakes filled the air, and a door clicked open on the far side of the cabin. The driver stepped down to the ground, his form illuminated in the headlights. He was short and stocky, with a thick beard. Dig recognised him as the forklift driver from the brewery.

The driver studied the branch, then blocked the glare of the headlight with one hand and studied the surrounding bushes. Dig ducked away amongst the foliage.

The driver scratched his face, then squatted and took hold of the branch. He dragged it roughly to the edge of the embankment and threw it over the side, shaking his head and mumbling to himself as he climbed the steps to the cabin.

Dig eased out of the bushes and scampered up the embankment, then ducked into the shadows behind the truck. The rail wheels had been lowered in the hybrid machine; the truck was balanced directly on the tracks.

The flatbed of the truck carried a large steel shipping container on the rear of the tray. A rectangle of space existed between the container and the driver's cabin—where a tangle of tarpaulin sheeting was roughly tied with flexible straps. Dig scurried along the side of the truck and hoisted himself up onto the bed, then crawled onto the tarpaulin sheeting and sat with his back against the container.

The driver pulled the door closed, and with a hiss of air the engine rumbled forward with a squeal of steel on steel. Dig braced himself against the container and held on. The hi-rail followed the tracks down over the rail bridge, then climbed the opposite side of the hill before settling into a steady pace as it drove toward Hampi.

As they neared town, the truck slowed and stopped. A whirring vibration emanated from below the truck tray, and the machine wobbled and settled into a new position before lurching sideways off the tracks. Dig recognised the familiar bounce of rubber wheels as they left the rail and rolled along the dirt road toward Hampi.

Soon after the truck turned onto a flat expanse of asphalt road. As it picked up speed the static roar of tyres on pavement filled the air. Streetlights flashed past like strobe lights.

If the truck was heading to the docks, then Dig planned to stay on the vehicle until it arrived. And if his bus journey over to Hampi was any indication, he guessed he would be on the truck until morning.

His eyes were sore, his head throbbed, he needed to sleep. But in front of him, between the cabin and the flatbed, was an open gap where the asphalt road raced below. If he fell forward while the truck was in motion he'd become roadkill.

He examined the tied tarpaulin sheeting below his rear, then pulled a frayed edge to reveal a dark sliver of space between the material and the metal truck bed. After considering for a moment, he lowered himself face down and pushed his way under the cloth.

Beneath the tarpaulin the air was oily and stale, and the hard metal flatbed was cold and pressed into his hips—but the straps over the sheeting held him in place and offered him a chance to sleep.

Dig hugged his pack to his chest and closed his eyes.

11

THE TRUCK LURCHED AND DIG shot upwards, then fell back to the metal of the truck bed with a jolt through his side. After a moment of disorientation between a fading dream and an unfamiliar reality—he pushed out from beneath the tarpaulin and stretched his neck.

His lower back was cramped and his lungs full of dust. He tried to clear his throat and fell into a coughing fit. When it relented, he sat up and rubbed his hip, willing the circulation back into his muscle.

The truck travelled down an asphalt road, flanked on both sides by a dense mass of palm trees and tropical shrubbery. The first light of the morning splintered through the branches. Water lay beside the roadway in open ditches, and the air was sticky and warm. He found his water and took a long drink.

The truck slowed and began to crunch back through the gears before veering into the dirt shoulder, where it came to a hissing stop. A tall advertising billboard faced the truck, partly concealed behind the palms.

A caption below the picture stated *Banyan Bitter – It's My Beer*. It depicted a slick-haired man holding a bottle. A pair of aviator sunglasses hung from his wide-collared shirt.

The driver opened his door and Dig heard the strains of bongos and a sitar. He scrambled under the tarpaulin before the man stepped down to the ground.

"Tanhai mein dil yaadein sanjota hai..." The driver placed one hand on the side of the cabin, unzipped his fly, and released a torrent of urine against the front wheel.

Dig lay still, barely covered by the tarpaulin and not three metres away from the driver as he watched his handiwork. If the man looked sideways, they would be face to face.

"Kya karoon haye, Koch Koch Hotai Hai..." the man sung as a steamy cloud of piss rose around him and floated up to Dig. He held his breath with a grimace. The urine fog smelt acrid, and the hairs inside his nose tickled and twitched, like an army of ants doing laps around his sinuses.

After a near impossible length of time the torrent reduced to a trickle, and then the trickle tapered down to a few short squirts. The driver gave a shake and wiped his hand on the seat of his trousers. He stepped across the gravel and thunked up the metal steps to the cabin.

A sneeze began building momentum in Dig's nose, and he clamped his mouth shut with his hand. It couldn't be suppressed, and when it finally exploded, it came out as a high pitched "Choo!" The driver's footfalls up the stairs stopped.

Dig squeezed his nostrils shut between his thumb and forefinger. The tickle slowly dissipated, and he allowed himself to breathe while watching the shadow of the driver beside the cab. There was a click, and the radio shut down abruptly—leaving a conspicuous silence, save for a whisper of wind in the palm fronds.

The shadow at the front of the truck moved, and a foot crunched back down to the gravel. The driver reappeared, facing the open road shoulder.

Dig lay still on the truck bed, his fingers clamped tightly over his nostrils, the fabric of the tarpaulin barely covering him.

The man took another two steps forward. His shoulders were bunched, and one arm hung stiffly at his side, grasping tightly what looked to be a small penknife. The tendons in his forearm bulged.

Behind him, a small bird of green and blue feathers floated down from the sky and landed on the top of the billboard. It stretched its wings, then gave a high pitched call.

The driver turned quickly toward the sound. After a moment the bird called again, and the driver's shoulders dropped and relaxed. He shook his head and muttered to himself.

The man pocketed the knife and climbed back up the stairs of the cabin. The door slammed shut and the muffled warble of the music returned. Moments later the engine crunched back into gear and they were moving again.

Dig took a deep breath and slid back out from beneath the tarpaulin. As the truck passed the billboard he watched the bird and frowned—unable to pinpoint a nagging sense of déjà vu.

The truck motored on at a steady pace as it climbed a hill, and trucks passed intermittently in the opposite direction, carrying containers. Eventually, the trees on the road shoulder made way for boxy concrete shacks with peeling paint. The road topped out on the peak of a vast headland, and Dig tasted the salty tang of the ocean in the slipstream.

In the distance to the left, a cluster of buildings crowded behind a long stretch of sandy beach. To the right lay a wide green harbour, banked by a line of steel cranes on the shore. A flat expanse of concrete spread behind the cranes, stacked with containers. Ships were parked in the harbour, ready to receive their cargo.

The docks, Dig thought, and pressed his lips together.

The road followed the ridge of the hill down toward the harbour. A chain link fence appeared beside the road, and the truck slowed to a crawl before it turned into a wide gate. A large, faded sign stood above it, announcing: MORMUGAO CONTAINER PORT, GOA

The truck rumbled through the gate and across the concrete, heading for the line of T-shaped cranes that stood on the harbour's edge like hulking rusted crucifixes. Beside them, trucks lined up across the carpark in rows. The Banyan Brewery vehicle rolled to a stop inside a faded white rectangle and awaited its turn to be unloaded.

As the cabin door clicked open, Dig lowered himself to the concrete on the opposite side, squatted, and crawled across the pavement until he found some cover beneath the tray of a nearby truck.

From here he could see the driver's feet as they shuffled around in front of the vehicle. A second set of hairy legs in shorts and sandals arrived beside him.

"You made it," said the owner of the sandals, in a strange accent. "Good trip?"

"Yes. There wasn't a lot of traffic."

"Well you're booked in for upload at nine thirty. So you've a couple of hours."

"Do you have the paperwork?"

"Aye, all here. And I've filled out the customs forms for ye, so you're ready to go."

"Good."

There was a flick of a lighter, and a puff of cigarette smoke rose into the sky. "Well, I'm out of here." The owner of the sandals sauntered off, back in the direction of the main road.

Dig crept after him, following at a distance, weaving through the maze of parked trucks. The man's blonde streaked hair hung to his shoulders, and strings of beaded bracelets were looped around his wrists.

The man exited the main gate of the dock and jogged across the road. When he reached the far side, he stepped down a sandy track that split through the trees and disappeared from sight.

Dig jogged across the road after him. A faded sign pointed down the sandy trail: *Baina Beach*. He followed.

The track snaked around the base of a rocky cliff and opened out onto a beach covered with coarse, brown sand. Waves broke along the shore, pushing clumps of seaweed onto the bank. A fine salty mist hung in the air. Dig stepped onto the sand and scanned the length of the beach—but it was empty. The guy had disappeared.

Behind the sand, a dirt road ran parallel to the shore, lined on both sides of the street with shops and stalls. The street was busy with people, and the warbled voice of an announcer filled the air. Dig paced toward the crowd.

It was a market, with wares packed tightly on both sides of the street. Spices were heaped on the ground in pointed piles, with vendors seated beside them. Foul smelling fish were lined up on tables, covered in flies. An elderly man stood before a vegetable stall, holding up a handful of greens as he haggled with the merchant. Shoulders jostled past him, and the hum of conversation filled the air.

Dig stood on his toes and scanned the crowd, then spotted the sandals guy by a motorbike halfway down the street. The guy lifted a roll of paper from the rear of the bike, stepped over to a plywood hoarding on the edge of the road, and tacked the paper billboard up on the wall. He returned to sit on the bike, and started it up.

Dig dodged through the horde. "Hey!" he shouted, and waved his arms. But the bike jerked forward and disappeared into the crowd.

Dig came to a stop beside the plywood hoarding, his hands on his hips. His brow furrowed and he slowly shook his head. After a moment he turned to look at the billboard the guy had fixed to the wall:

THE BANYAN BREWHOUSE
HOME OF BANYAN BITTER
SUNDOWN PARTY
EVERY NIGHT TILL LATE
RESIDENT DJ
FREE ENTRY
CLIFFTOP ROAD, ANJUNA
SEE YOU THERE!

Dig blinked and reread the sign. He looked up and down the market, before his attention turned to a woman who sat cross legged on the ground. She wore gold hooped earrings, and supported a double chin over a patterned dress. Heavy sacks were stacked on the road beside her, brimming with dark red, knobbly sausages.

"Excuse me," Dig said, pointing to the sign. "Is Anjuna far from here?"

The woman studied the sign, then wobbled her head. "About an hour," she said. "To drive."

"Okay." Dig pursed his lips and glanced back up the road. "Are there any taxis around here? Or rickshaws?"

She frowned and shook her head. "You going to Anjuna?"

"Yes."

"Ah." Her eyes lit up, and she turned toward a dark concrete room in the building behind her. "Rakesh!"

A pot-bellied man with a bald head walked out of the darkness. The couple had a quick discussion in Hindi, then the man turned to Dig.

"Hello," he said. "Where you from?"

"Australia."

"Ah! David Warner and Mitchell Johnson. Good cricketers."

"They are," said Dig, smiling.

"Where you going?"

"I'm trying to get to Anjuna."

The man nodded. "Okay then. Come with me." He gestured toward the back room.

"Are you a taxi driver?"

The man frowned. "No," he said. "I make chouricos."

Dig looked at him blankly, and the man pointed to the sacks of dried sausage stacked in front of the woman. "Goan sausage."

"Is that like chorizo?"

"Yes, but better." The man grinned and waved his hand again. "Come on. I've a delivery to make in Anjuna. You can come with me. No problem."

Dig blinked. "Oh right...thanks."

The man entered the building. Lengths of the knobbly red sausage hung from floor to ceiling in rows. A doorway at the rear of the room led to an alleyway and a rusted, three wheeled vehicle. The front cabin of the machine was small and enclosed. A flat steel tray filled the rear of the machine, making the vehicle look like a cross between a motorbike and a tiny pick-up truck.

"My auto rickshaw," the man said. "You can squeeze in the back." Stacked tightly in the rear tray were wide circular sacks, brimming with chouricos. Dig raised his eyebrows.

"Have you tried chouricos before?"

"No."

"Well come on then!" The man snapped a handful of the sausage off the top of the nearest pile and held it out. "Try!"

Dig took the chouricos; it was soft and knobbly in his hand, like a string of oversized rosary beads, and the colour of dried blood. "Is it cooked?"

"Of course. By the sun. We leave it outside for three months."

"You just leave it on the ground? Raw?"

"Well...yes. It's raw at first. But it's dried out now." The man gestured to the sausage in Dig's hand. "You see?"

Dig glanced from the chouricos to the rickshaw, his lips thin. The man watched him with an expectant smile.

Dig shrugged, then brought the meat to his mouth and took a bite. It was chewy, and strong flavours of pork, garlic and vinegar soon gave way to a burning chilli fire. His eyes widened, and his mouth dropped open. "Whoah, it's bloody hot."

The man laughed.

"Not bad though."

"You see?"

Dig nodded. "Why's it so knobbly anyway?"

"That's just the natural shape of the pig intestine."

The chouricos caught in Dig's throat, and he coughed, fighting down a retch. He forced a smile, and swallowed it down. It felt like he was trying to swallow a golf ball.

"Shall we go?"

"Yes," Dig said, nodding slowly. "Let's go."

He climbed onto the back tray and squeezed between the sacks to sit with his back against the cab. The pungent odour of the chouricos surrounded him. The rickshaw vibrated into life and bounced down the lane into the open road. His stomach flipped over and acid rose into the back of his throat, but he tried to put it out of his mind.

12

THE TRIP WAS BUMPY AND LONG, but eventually the engine dropped down to a puttering rumble as the machine came to a halt. They were parked in a thin dirt road with tightly packed restaurants crowded on both sides.

"Anjuna," Rakesh shouted.

Dig pushed through the sacks to the street and stretched his back. "Thanks for the lift." He reached for his wallet.

"No! That's fine. In fact, here..." Rakesh grabbed another handful of sausage from the vehicle. "Take some more chouricos for lunch."

Dig paused, then took it from him. "Um, thanks."

"No problem." Rakesh returned to the driver's seat. "Have a good trip." The engine revved into life and the rickshaw accelerated away down the street. Dig looked down at the sausage in his hand, frowned, and pocketed it.

At his feet, a rooster pecked through a pile of food scraps. Two deeply tanned girls with blonde, braided hair walked past him in long skirts and singlet tops. A guy with a crewcut and a covering of tattoos from neck to waist weaved a moped down the street. Somewhere behind him, the pulse of dance music resonated.

Dig walked toward the sound. The road climbed up, and as it approached the top of a rise, a large dirt carpark appeared, filled with motorbikes. Beside it stood a wide, double-storey building, covered in vines and blinking fairy lights. The thump of bass resonated over an underlying rumble of conversation. An illuminated sign hung from the roof, announcing: *The Banyan Brewhouse. Sundown Party Tonight!*

The building sat on top of a high cliff, with coastal views in both directions. An onshore breeze whipped up over the cliff edge and cooled Dig's arms; seagulls with dirty brown wings circled above his head.

He entered through a rear beer garden, weaving his way through groups of westerners with deep tans and unkempt hair, talking and smoking at the tables that lined the cliff edge.

The beer garden led into a wide room of natural timber columns and exposed ceilings. Curtains of glass beads dropped over a floor of tightly compacted dirt. Here, westerners crowded shoulder-to-shoulder in a dense haze, smoking and drinking. The music pounded around the room, and as he passed two speakers that were taller than him, he felt the thump of the bass resonate in his chest cavity.

He moved further inside, and the room morphed into a dark, heaving dancefloor. Rows of fluorescent blue lights hung from the ceiling—the type that made your teeth glow bright. The crowd was dancing, punching the air and turning erratic circles over the floor. Up in the corner of the room, a sweaty-faced DJ stood in a booth, nodding his head and working the decks in front of him.

Dig pushed his way through the crowd. He sidestepped a tall, bearded guy staring at the ceiling with his hands linked behind his head. A girl with dark makeup and dropped eyelids turned circles beside him, pointing at the crowd like she was conducting an orchestra. Dig sidled past her into the path of a solid guy in a tight green T-shirt with *Banyan Bitter* emblazoned across it. He held a beer bottle diagonally at his chest and stared listlessly at the ground. Liquid dribbled from the neck of the bottle and tracked down his shirt.

Dig spotted a bar at the back of the room. He pushed through the pack, and when he reached it he leaned back against the counter.

A guy sat on a seat beside him, reading a paper. A necklace of shells hung around his neck, partially concealed by his shoulder length, sun bleached hair. Dig took an intake of breath as he realised he was the same guy he had seen earlier at the docks.

The guy's eyebrows knitted and he turned to look at Dig with bloodshot eyes.

Dig pursed his lips; he realised he had been staring. "Hey," he shouted, and nodded.

The guy nodded back to him, then returned to his paper.

Dig blinked and rubbed at the back of his neck. "Pretty busy in here huh?"

The guy looked Dig up and down before speaking. "It was a lot worse a few hours ago. You just arrived?"

"Yeah. Can you tell?"

The guy smirked and shrugged.

Dig pointed to the beer taps. "Banyan Bitter huh? I see this advertised a lot. Any good?"

"Why don't you give it a try."

Dig pointed to the empty space on the bar in front of the guy. "You aren't drinking?"

"Just finished work." He closed his paper. "But I could be swayed." He waved his arm at a girl who stood at the opposite end of the bar, and she walked over to them. She had wide green eyes, high cheekbones, and flowing brown and blonde streaked hair that hung to her waist in a tangled collection, intertwined with braids and beads. Her small green singlet top supported an ample cleavage.

"Two green labels please," the guy said.

She squatted down to retrieve two bottled beers from a fridge, and Dig fought the urge to glance at her cleavage for the second time. She lifted the beers to the bar and whipped off the tops with a flick of the wrist. A surge of bubbles rose from the opening and tracked down the neck of the frosted glass. The green label read *Banyan Bitter*.

"Cheers." They clinked their bottles together and drank. Dig was thirsty, and he gulped down two long mouthfuls. It tasted good, yet also very familiar; he looked at the bottle, trying to pinpoint the nagging feeling of déjà vu.

"You alright?" the guy said.

Then clarity hit him. The beer tasted the same as the signature drink from the Buckley Brewery, the *Buckley's Chance*. This was logical of course, as they were fermented from the same crop of hops.

Dig glanced up, his concentration broken. "Yeah fine. Just tastes like a beer I know back home." He held out his hand. "My name's Dig anyway."

The guy looked at Dig's hand, then reached out to shake it. "Most people call me Chook."

Dig pointed to a seat beside him. "Mind if I sit?" The guy shook his head, and Dig sat down. "So you work here? At the bar?"

"Sort of."

"Seems like a cool place to work."

The guy frowned. "If you like incoherent drunks, then sure." He took another sip of his beer. "You Australian then?"

"Yeah. You?"

"Irish."

"Nice." The girl behind the bar served a couple more people, reaching down below the counter for more bottles of the green labelled beer. She wore a flowing skirt and no shoes.

After a moment, Dig turned his attention away from her. Chook met his gaze with raised eyebrows.

"Sorry," Dig said. "I got a bit distracted there."

The girl returned to their side of the bar.

"Dig," Chook said. "This is my sister, Jules."

"Hi," Jules said, smiling.

Dig blinked rapidly. "Good to meet you."

Chook smirked, then turned back to his sister. "How's the day going?"

"The usual shit." She tucked a strand of hair behind her ear. "One guy fell asleep on the toilet; a spaced-out chick decided to try to pierce her own nipple up in the DJ booth; and a mumbling freak who looks like Frankenstein keeps trying to touch me." She wiped the top of the bar with a furry green tea towel. "You know, just a normal morning."

Chook nodded.

A group of guys approached the bar and Jules headed over to serve them. Dig turned to Chook. "Hey," he whispered. "About what I said."

"Ha, don't worry about it. Just wanted to see you squirm."

Dig took another sip on his beer. "Sounds like you guys have been in Goa a while?"

Chook shrugged. "Six months for me. She's been here about a year."

"You plan to stay a while then?"

"Not really. I'm only here because my sister's here." He took a mouthful. "I'm trying to get her to head home with me."

"She won't go?"

He shook his head. "She's caught up in this whole...scene...you know, getting into too many drugs and hanging with some dodgy people."

"So how'd you guys get jobs here then?"

Chook took another mouthful. "My sis is screwing the arsehole that runs this place."

A shout came from the opposite end of the room. One of the customers leaned over the bar and reached for Jules. He was tall and solid, with short cropped hair on a boxy head. His eyes were heavily lidded. He did indeed look like a demented version of Frankenstein.

"Get away!" Jules slapped at his hand.

Chook pushed to his feet with his eyes narrowed, and Frankenstein's two friends dragged him away to the dancefloor.

Jules strode across the bar to Chook; her face was red. "Can you watch the bar for a bit? I'm gettin' security."

"Not sure I have the cleavage for it. But I'll give it a shot."

She gave a pinched expression, picked up the damp towel from the bench, and threw it at him. He tried to duck away, but it slapped into the side of his head and fell back to the bar. She crossed the room toward a staircase in the corner. Dig watched her go.

"Right! Time to work." Chook moved behind the bar, before putting on a deep stilted voice and furrowing his brow. "Sorry sir but I can't serve you. You've obviously had way too much to drink. Don't want you falling asleep on the toilet now."

"Ha ha." Dig lifted the towel from the bar and feigned to throw it. Chook ducked and smiled, showing a set of crooked teeth. He grabbed his beer and swallowed a mouthful.

"So what brings you over here anyway?" Chook said.

Dig picked at the label of his beer. "Work."

"Work? You in tourism?"

"I work in a brewery actually."

"Ha! Come to learn from the masters huh? I bet you don't get beers like this back in Australia." He tapped the top of his bottle.

Dig shrugged. "One of our beers tastes pretty much the same. We use the same hops actually."

Chook frowned. "I'm not talking about the *taste* dude."

Dig looked up. "Huh?"

Chook gestured to the dance floor. "Why'd you think this place is so packed every night? And so full of spaced-out twats?"

Dig straightened. "What do you mean?"

Chook leaned forward and pointed to Dig's beer. "The green label's the local stuff. They only sell it in this bar. They call it *unrefined.*"

Dig's stomach clenched. He lifted the beer and studied the label. "Unrefined?"

Chook glanced over his shoulder to the stairwell. "Look, don't tell anyone I said this, but I think they have, like, genetically modified the hops somehow. You know, with *science*. Infused them with, like, opium poppies to make some kind of hybrid, alien plant." He picked up his bottle and presented it like he was doing a magic trick. "So when they brew it—ta daa!"

"Opium?" Dig's breath caught in his chest and his mind raced.

He thought back to the crop fields in Hampi—the endless rows of hops with the strange orange tinge, and Girish's doctorate in Botany sitting proudly framed on his wall. Then the containers of the 'secret' hops that were delivered to the Buckley Brewery every month, and the block of material that Shiv had regularly arranged to pick up from his father.

Had his father been extracting the opium out of the hops?

The final words from his father came back to him. The words choked out as he lay stricken on the bush track, his throat closing up, drowning him of oxygen:

The brewery is tainted...you should shut it down...no more packages.

Dig's heart pounded as he stared at the beer in his hand. A tinkling crash echoed behind him, and he turned to see Frankenstein in the middle of the dancefloor, swaying left and right as he yanked a curtain of beads down from the ceiling.

"Man," Chook said. "That guy's lost the plot. Shiv needs to get down here now."

Dig turned quickly. "Did you say Shiv?"

Chook gave a blank look. "Yeah, he's Jules' boyfriend. You know him? He's a right prick huh?" He joined his thumb and forefinger in a circle and waggled it at his forehead—the universal symbol of a dickhead. "But even so, he'll make that guy wish he never set foot in here." He turned to the staircase. "All good. Here they come now."

Across the room, Jules appeared in the stairway with Shiv and the thugs behind her. Dig's chest tightened. "I've got to get out of here." He stood up. His stool thumped to the floor behind him.

Chook frowned. "Hey, chill—"

"Gotta go." Dig turned for the exit. His hand brushed against his beer bottle, and it dropped to the floor and shattered, covering his toes in beer and glass. Dig stared at his feet for a long moment—it was somehow hard to comprehend, like his thought process was battling through a numbing cloud of fog. His balance wavered, and he reached for the bar to steady himself.

There it is, Dig thought. *The opium's kicking in.* He swallowed, took a deep breath, then glanced across the room. Shiv stared at him from the base of the staircase, eyes wide. Dig began to stumble across the dancefloor toward the exit.

"Hey Dig!" Chook shouted from somewhere behind him, somewhere far away. "Wait a sec!"

But Dig pushed on. The pulsing lights of the dancefloor danced in his vision, throwing shadows, disorientating him. The bass pounded in his temples. He blinked, trying to focus on the fuzzy shapes before his eyes, but they swayed left and right like cartoon ghosts. Something slammed into his chest, and he fell to his rear on the dirt floor.

A figure dropped to the ground beside him, and he turned to see Frankenstein lying on his side, scowling. "You idiot," the guy slurred.

"Sorry." Dig pulled himself to his feet. His legs were shaky, his head full of cotton wool. He pushed onward through the crowd, bumping against shoulders until he recognised the bright rectangle of the exit. He moved toward the light, and as he reached the door, a figure appeared before him.

"Leaving so soon?" Shiv said. His eyes were steely.

Dig turned back inside, but the thugs stood behind him, blocking his path. He faced Shiv again and steadied himself on the door frame.

"I've decided to take your advice and head home," Dig said. "All hush hush and all that. Never see each other again. Just like you said back in Oz."

Shiv clenched his teeth and placed an arm against the frame, blocking it. "It's a bit late for that."

Dig glanced around at the three men. "No...it's okay, I better hit the road I think. Long flight back." He pushed forward and tried to duck under Shiv's arm.

Shiv shifted his body to block his path. "You need to come upstairs."

Dig tried to smile, and pushed forward again. "Maybe next time."

A hand came down tightly on Dig's shoulder, turning him. Another pressed into the small of his back, pushing him back toward the bar.

"Okay," Dig said. "Maybe I'll just say hello, seeing as I'm here."

He was directed through the dancefloor toward the stairs in the back corner of the room. As they passed the bar, Chook frowned.

"No Shiv! That's not him! That blockhead down there's the problem." He pointed at Frankenstein, who hadn't yet managed to stand up.

"Chook," Dig shouted as he was pushed across the room. "Don't worry about it."

Chook stepped forward and grabbed Shiv's arm. "Shiv, you have the wrong guy."

Shiv scowled. "Get your hands off me."

"Just *listen* for once you dickhead. This guy isn't the problem. He was sitting with me quietly at the bar."

"Chook, stop it!" Jules said from behind him.

Shiv grabbed a handful of Chook's shirt and shoved him to the ground. Chook fell back to his elbows with his chest rising and falling and his cheeks blushed pink. Shiv nodded to his companions, and they pushed Dig onward toward the stairs.

A rush of footsteps skipped across the floor behind them and Chook punched Shiv in the jaw. Shiv fell to one knee with a hand at his face and his lip smeared with blood. Chook stood over him, fists at his side, eyes wide.

The thick-jawed thug took two quick steps and backhanded Chook across the face with a slap, then swung a punch into the pit of his stomach. Chook buckled over in a heap.

Jules squealed and rushed to Chook's side. "What the hell are you doing?" she screamed at the thug.

Shiv nodded to the stairs, and the thug grabbed Chook by the collar, dragging him across the floor.

"No!" Jules pulled at the thug's elbow, but he hardly noticed her.

Dig took a final glance toward the dancefloor, but nobody in the crowd seemed to have noticed what was happening—they were staring vacantly at the DJ.

The hand in Dig's back pushed him upward, and he watched his feet as he stumbled up the timber steps. Over time, foot falls had worn depressions in the centre of the risers. He concentrated on placing each foot in the centre of the step, one at a time, trying not to stumble as he battled the murky fog that had descended over his mind.

When they reached the upper level, the stairs opened out to a dusty room with a leather couch wedged against one wall, and an empty bar on the other. An elevator shaft lay open in the corner, blocked off with tape, and double doors led to a balcony that overlooked the beer garden below. The thump of bass reverberated up from the dancefloor.

The thugs pushed Dig and Chook down to the couches. Jules took a seat beside her brother and sat stiffly with her arms crossed. "Shiv, this is bullshit."

"Leave it."

"No! Let Chook go back down."

"Keep your mouth shut!" Shiv shouted, and Jules cringed, then opened her mouth to speak before closing it again.

Dig perched on the front edge of the seat. He was still struggling to process his thoughts, but willed his concentration through it. "Is Max here?" he said. "I want to speak to him."

Shiv put a hand on his hip, then smirked at the bald-headed thug. "Oh, you want to speak to him do you?"

Dig blinked around the room. "Yes."

Shiv snorted and the thugs laughed. "No, you can't speak to *him*."

"Look. Just give me five minutes—"

"Dig!" Chook interrupted. "I don't know what you think you're doing, but Max isn't a dude."

Dig looked blankly at Chook. "Well what is...he?"

"Her real name's Maxine. But everyone calls her Max."

Shiv laughed, then walked to a doorway near the staircase and knocked lightly against the frame. "We've got a visitor."

Chook rubbed at his neck and gave Jules a pained look. They shuffled closer to each other on the couch, their lips thin.

A patter of tiny footsteps approached from the doorway, and an overweight bulldog waddled through the door with its tongue hanging sideways. It trotted over to a worn basket of blankets near the balcony and plopped itself down.

Behind it, a short, stocky woman walked into the room, wearing a draping brown sari and her hair tied tightly at the back of her head. She held a cigarette in her hand, and the sickening smell of cloves filled the air. She scowled at the three people sitting on the couch. "So," she said in a gravelly voice through brown stained teeth. "You just couldn't keep away." She lifted the cigarette and took a drag.

Dig's mind churned. He thought back to the voice he had spoken to on the phone in Australia. He had assumed it was male from the deep tone. But it seemed he was wrong.

And she looked somehow familiar. His brow furrowed. It was hard to keep a grip on his thoughts.

Shiv stepped toward Maxine. "Would you like a drink?"

She nodded, and the thick-jawed thug opened a fridge behind the bar.

Dig stood up. "Look—"

"Sit," she said.

Dig paused, then sat back down on the edge of the couch. "Look," he repeated. "We aren't meeting in the best circumstances here, but I think we need to talk."

"Yes," Maxine gave a cold smile. "I agree with you. Please go ahead."

Dig cleared his throat before speaking. "The thing is," he said in a shaky voice. "I originally came to India to try to talk to you guys about our old hop supply deal back in Australia. But now I'm here, I've changed my mind." He glanced over to Shiv. "Shiv and I talked back home about closing things down. And I actually think that's a good idea now. No more Banyan hops. No more Buckley's Chance. Call it quits."

Maxine stood stiffly with a downturned mouth. Smoke drifted out of her nose and billowed in the air.

Dig swallowed. "So, I think the best thing we can do is just forget I came here at all, and I'll keep quiet, go home, and never talk to you guys again. No harm done." He held up his hands and tried to smile.

Maxine watched him with a deadpan expression, before emitting a *humph*. She walked over to dog's basket, squatted down, and ruffled the skin behind the animal's neck. "Did you hear that Digit? The stickybeak's decided he's going to let himself leave." The dog's ears pricked up. "That's funny isn't it!" she said, and turned to Dig. "So you decide to travel over here, snoop about our factories and businesses—then announce you're going home again, taking all our company secrets with you?"

Dig pursed his lips. "That's *not* why I came here. I came here to talk to *you*." He glanced from Maxine to Shiv. "You have to understand, Dad's death left us completely in the dark about the future of our brewery. Without your hops, we're ruined." He swallowed. "But I realise that's how it has to be now. Let's just forget everything, and we'll never even think about you guys again."

"Forget everything?" Maxine's voice raised an octave. "Yeah sure, I'll just forget the guy that sneaks into my private property, then enters my house and tries to break up my family?"

Dig frowned, then recognition dawned. That was why Maxine had seemed familiar—she was the lady he had seen on the wall of Raj's house near the brewery. She was the boy's mother.

"No..." He shook his head. "You've got that wrong. If that's true...then I didn't even know it was your house. I was *invited* into it."

She gave another *humph*, and squatted back down to pat the dog. She spoke slowly. "You and your family...have always been...problems. And I don't like problems." The dog turned and offered the underside of his neck, and she duly scratched it. "Shiv told me how much of a problem your brother was. He also told me that he screamed like a baby when he sliced him up." She leaned closer to the animal. "Do you remember that finger Digit? It wasn't very tasty was it? It was a bit rotten, travelling all that way from Australia. But you ate it all the same." She smirked. "Don't worry, we'll get you a fresh one...just before we take the stickybeak on a nice fishing trip." She stroked the dog's forehead. "Do you think he'll scream too? I think he will. He's no more than a weak child, living under the faded shadow of a weak father."

Dig's heart raced, and a flush crept up his neck to pound in his ears. His hands balled into fists. He clenched his teeth and forced a deep breath.

He glanced toward the stairs, but they were blocked by the thugs. Shiv stood in the doorway to the balcony. Would anyone hear him if he shouted? He doubted it. The thumping bass from the dancefloor still resonated around them.

"Look," Dig said. "Whatever deal you had with my father, I can replicate it. I know the hops are bioengineered with the opium poppies. I realise my father was extracting the opium during the brewing process and giving it to you in Australia. I can figure out how to do that for you. You have my word. No problems."

Maxine took another drag on her cigarette and gave a pinched expression. The thick-jawed thug handed her a bottle of beer. She took a large mouthful. "I can't trust my business to a couple of insolent kids." She cocked her head. "But, I'd love to hear how you came to your insightful conclusion about how we engineer our crops."

Chook shifted in his seat beside Dig.

"I...just guessed it."

"You just guessed?" Maxine sneered. "Or did somebody *tell* you while you were sitting at the bar? It wouldn't be the first time that's happened." Chook dropped his gaze to the floor.

Maxine turned to Shiv. "What happened to your mouth?"

There was a pause, before Chook spoke up. "I punched him," he said. "But I'm sorry. I shouldn't have done that. It looks like there's stuff going on here I didn't know about."

"So what are we going to do about that?"

"Look," Shiv said as he glanced at Jules. "He was wrong. But he didn't understand the history."

"No! Tell me again. What are we going to do?"

Shiv swallowed. "Punish him."

"Good." Maxine's eyes lit up. "This'll be a reminder of what happens when you bring outsiders into the business. Especially the ones related to dirty western *sluts*. You get...problems."

"Please," Chook said. "I won't do it again."

"No you won't. Because you'll remember this moment every time you pick your nose."

Chook's eyebrows knitted together, and he exchanged a look with his sister. Jules sat up straight in her chair. "Max, you don't need to do that."

"I suggest you keep your mouth shut tramp, as you're the one who brought him here."

Jules turned to Shiv, her eyes pleading. His forehead creased and he stared at the floor.

"Shiv?" Maxine raised her eyebrows.

Shiv blinked, then after a moment he shuffled across to the bar, pulled open a drawer, and extracted a pair of pruning shears. The silver blades glinted in the light, and looked razor sharp.

"No!" Jules stood with a hand on her hip. "Shiv! Stop it!"

Shiv flinched.

Chook leapt from his seat and ran for the stairs, but the bald-headed thug tackled him to the ground, placed a knee in his back, and twisted his arm backwards.

"Do it," Maxine said. "Now."

Shiv clenched his jaw and moved across to kneel beside Chook.

Jules ran at him. She only managed a few steps before the thick-jawed thug caught her around the waist and dragged her backwards. "Let...me...go!" she shouted, and flailed at his arms. Chook struggled on the floor, wriggling and grunting, trying to free himself.

"Please Shiv," Jules sobbed.

Maxine stood beside Shiv. The smoke from her cigarette wafted into his face. "Do it."

Chook moaned as the thug yanked his arm up into the small of his back.

"If you do it we're over," Jules screamed, and Shiv momentarily closed his eyes. The hand that held the pruning shears was shaking, and it faltered to his side. For a second all were still.

Maxine sighed. "You stupid boy." She stepped forward and pushed her cigarette into the side of Shiv's cheek. There was a sizzling sound, and Shiv flinched away in a grimace. The stench of burning flesh filled the air. Maxine snarled again. "Do it!"

Shiv nodded. His lips were thin as he lifted the shears to Chook's finger, and squeezed the handles together.

There was a crunching sound and Chook howled. The men released their hold and he rolled to one side, clutching at his hand. Blood was smeared across the floor in a crimson arc, and at the end of it, a bloodied finger lay forlorn in the centre of the tiles.

Jules was released, and she ran across the room to her brother and hugged him, burying her head in his shoulder. "I'm…sorry," she sobbed.

Dig sat frozen in his seat. A mouthful of bile threatened to rise in his throat, but he fought it down.

Maxine delicately retrieved the finger from the floor, and held it up to the light. "There. That should remind you to keep strangers out of our business."

Chook sat huddled on the floor, supporting his arm, his chest rising and falling rapidly.

Maxine grinned and hummed under her breath. She turned to the dog by the door. "Digit!" she exclaimed in a high pitched voice. "I have a *snackie* for you!" The dog pricked up its ears. "*Fin-gers!*" she sung in a melodic tone, waggling the appendage in the air.

The dog trotted across the room to sit obediently beside Maxine. "See?" she said, and held the finger down to the dog. "A nice fresh one." The dog lifted its head and plucked the finger from her grasp. It chewed twice, then tipped its head back and swallowed it, before licking its lips and cocking its head.

"You sick bitch," Jules sobbed.

Maxine patted the dog's head. "You still hungry? Well that's okay. We still have a few snackies left for you. In fact, our Australian visitor won't be needing any fingers in the near future."

She turned to Shiv. "It's his turn."

Shiv looked up, blank-faced and bleary eyed. He nodded, and the thick-jawed thug sidled toward Dig on the couch.

Dig stood up. His heart thumped and adrenaline coursed through his veins. He looked around the room, searching for an escape, but his path to the stairs and balcony were blocked. A hand clamped around his elbow. His eyes turned to the open lift shaft, and he took a quick intake of breath. He knew what to do.

He jammed a hand into his pocket and fished around inside. His hand eventually grasped what he was looking for, and he held it tightly.

The thug dragged Dig to the centre of the room and dumped him face first onto the tile. A knee pressed into his back, and a sickly, wet warmth soaked into his midriff; Dig guessed he was lying in Chook's blood.

Maxine stood over him, smiling. Her cigarette dangled from her hand. The dog sat beside her, its tongue lolling in time with its breath. Shiv knelt beside Dig, shears ready.

Dig met Maxine's eyes for a moment, then he turned to the animal.

"*Digit!*" he said, mimicking Maxine's high pitched voice from earlier. "*Fin-gers!*" He extracted his prize from his pocket—the piece of dried chouricos sausage from his trip over to Anjuna, and threw it across the room.

The sausage bounced once, then skidded across the tile, tracking through the smear of blood before it came to a stop at the edge of the lift shaft.

The dog bound up and ran across the room, chasing the sausage, its claws clicking over the tiled floor.

"Digit!" Maxine shouted. "Come here!" But the dog kept going, scurrying across the floor. As it approached the sausage it pushed its front paws out to stop. But, instead of halting, the paws landed in the pool of blood and the animal slid forward across the tile.

"Stop him!" Maxine screamed, but it was too late. The dog skated across the bloodied floor with its ears pinned back to its head, turning clockwise as it scrambled for purchase on the wet tile. It reached the edge of the shaft, tipped backwards over the drop, and disappeared.

"Digit! Mummy's coming!" Maxine ran to the shaft, the fat on her hips jiggling through the fabric of her sari as she moved. She reached the opening and knelt down. "Are you okay?" A pained howl echoed from deep within the shaft.

Maxine turned quickly. "Come on!" she shouted at the thug holding Dig. "Go get him!"

Dig felt the grip on his neck release and the thick-jawed thug ran for the stairs and disappeared. The bald-headed man moved to the stairway entrance, blocking it.

Dig pushed himself to his feet and glanced around the room. "Come on!" he shouted to Jules and Chook, and ran for the balcony.

Shiv's eyes widened and he dashed to the balcony doorway, trying to block Dig's exit.

Dig ran straight at him, clenched his teeth and dropped his shoulder forward, slamming Shiv in the centre of the chest. He sent him crashing into the bar with a clatter of broken glass.

Dig pushed through the balcony doorway and skidded to a stop at the handrail. He surveyed the beer garden below, a collection of plastic chairs and tables amongst gnarled trees and waist-high brick walls. The tables were half occupied, and beer bottles were strewn across the surfaces. Dig grasped the handrail and hoisted himself over the edge.

He dropped through the air and landed on a table. It imploded under his weight, spraying beer bottles to the floor. Something hard ripped at his lower back before he thumped into the ground.

Jules' feet dangled above him before she dropped. He pushed to his knees and tried to support her fall, but her rear caught him across the shoulder, knocking him back to the ground. He took a couple of ragged breaths.

Chook crashed down to his left, pulverising another plastic table full of bottles, then lay on his back, eyes squinted in pain, cradling his hand.

Dig scampered over to him, pulling him to his feet. "Let's go!" Chook nodded, and Dig slung Chook's arm around his neck and dragged him toward the car park.

"Keys," Chook panted. "My pocket." Dig reached into Chook's pants pocket and removed a key tied to a strip of leather.

As they reached the car park, Chook pointed to a battered trail bike. The three squeezed together on the seat, with Dig at the helm, Jules behind him, and Chook at the rear. The seat buckled under their combined weight as they sat down. Dig turned the key in the ignition and the bike roared to life.

From behind them, Shiv burst through the outside door of the bar, breathing hard. He spotted them and ran.

"Go!" screamed Jules. Dig looked down at the pedals on the bike. He pressed a backward lever and it clunked into gear.

"Can you drive this thing?" she shouted.

"I'm learning!" Dig released the clutch. The motor screamed and the bike jerked forward, lifting the front wheel from the ground before it thumped back down. Dig wrestled the controls straight again and steered the bike toward the main road. As they passed over a pothole the rear wheel guard bottomed out with a crunch.

Dig pulled back the throttle, heading out of town. The bike strained under the combined weight of the three passengers, and Jules clung tightly to Dig's midriff.

"Where to?" Dig shouted.

"The railway station," Chook screamed. "Just keep going straight."

"My place first," Jules said.

"No time!"

"Just give me thirty seconds. It's just up here—that white building."

Dig furrowed his brow. "Shouldn't we just go?"

Jules pulled in close behind him; the swell of her breasts pushed up against his back. She spoke into his ear. "Please, just let me get my bag."

Dig swallowed, blinked, and steered the bike off the road, bringing it to a stop outside the boxy concrete building. Thick mesh barred its windows. Jules jumped down from the bike.

"Shit Jules!" Chook said. "Hurry up!"

She jogged to the front porch and fumbled some keys into a lock, then swung open a heavy metal door before disappearing inside.

Dig looked to the road behind him, scanning for any signs of Shiv or his friends. He rapidly tapped his foot on the ground. "Come on," he said under his breath.

Moments later, Jules burst through the door again, carrying a multi-coloured, hand woven bag. She left the door open behind her as she ran across the drive and jumped back onto the bike. Dig accelerated back out onto the road.

The road was long and flat, and cut through long stretches of rainforest and palm trees. Dig drove as fast as the bike would allow. He squinted and ducked his head forward as moisture from his watering eyes tracked back across his face. Jules sat close behind him, arms tightly around his waist. He imagined Chook on the back end of the machine, likely holding onto the rear frame of the bike with only one hand, the other cradled against his chest.

After some time, small brick shacks began to appear on the side of the street, and the road narrowed into a level crossing over a railway line. A set of open boom gates stood on both sides of the track. Beside it was a platform and station building.

"Left here," Chook said, pointing to a dirt alleyway that disappeared behind a row of buildings. Dig pulled into the alleyway, and brought the bike to a stop beside a set of rusted steps. Dig killed the engine and kicked up the bike stand.

Chook was off the bike first, and he stumbled over to sit on the bottom riser of the steps. His face was pale; his injured hand still cradled on his chest. Blood ran down his arm to his elbow. He reached into a pocket with his good arm and produced a packet of cigarettes. As he fumbled out a cigarette with a shaking hand the box fell to the ground and bounced away. He watched it falter to a stop, then grimaced and closed his eyes.

Jules stepped down from the bike and walked over to Chook. "Arms up," she said, then grabbed his T-shirt and lifted it over his head. She wiped the blood from his arm and tied the T-shirt tightly around his injured hand.

She crouched and lifted the cigarette box from the ground, shook out a cigarette and placed it in Chook's mouth, then extracted a lighter from inside the box, and flicked a flame into life. The end of the cigarette glowed orange as it fired up. Jules sat beside him on the step.

"How's the hand?"

Chook rolled his glassy eyes. "Sore."

"We need to get you to a hospital."

"Not in Goa. That's the first place they'll look." He clenched his teeth as another wave of pain overtook him. "I think there's a train due, heading north. We'll find somewhere up there."

"Can you wait that long?"

"I'll have to."

Dig cleared his throat. "Hey Chook." He scratched the back of his neck. "I'm sorry about your hand. I...feel like it was my fault."

Chook gave a weak shrug. "At least we're finally away from that place." He turned back to his sister. "What did you take from the house?"

"Don't worry about it. Just clothes, and some money."

"No gear?"

Jules frowned. "No."

"You sure? Because if you stole any of Shiv's stash you better dump it right here."

"I told you I didn't. So leave it."

Chook watched her for a moment then turned his attention to the train station. The entrance was filling up with people—milling in groups and squatting on the floor. "After I get my hand sorted we're flying home. Back to Ireland. Right?"

She studied her fingernails and gave an almost imperceptible nod.

A low rumble approached from the distance and a dirty silver train laboured into the station, belching smoke and sounding its horn. It slowed to a stop with a hiss of brakes, and the passengers crowded around the doors.

"Let's go."

They picked up their packs and jogged out into the street, dodging motor rickshaws and taxis until they reached the busy station lobby. People jostled for space around them.

They pushed out onto the platform, and headed for a door of the train. A porter offered to take their bags from them, but they waved him away. A dirty faced boy clasped packets to his chest and yelled "Pea...nuts!" into the open windows of the train. Behind him a man held a tray above his head, balancing glass cups filled with milky liquid. "Chai! Chai!" he cried in a low drone. They followed the tide of people into the train, and crouched inside the doorway.

Dig bit his lip and looked across the platform to the street. Disembarking passengers streamed out across the dirt road, loading bags into rickshaws and lining up in front of buses. He took a sharp intake of breath as a motorbike screamed around the corner and skidded to a halt beside the station. Shiv dropped the bike to the ground and strode toward the train. Two more motorbikes appeared behind him with the silhouettes of the thugs in the seats.

"They're coming," Dig said.

Jules' eyes widened. "Oh shite."

"Get down."

Somewhere a whistle blew, and with a shudder the train moved forward. Through the open door they watched the platform creep away beside them. They hunkered low in the carriage until it rolled past the station building. Shiv stood in the forecourt, hands on hips, breathing heavily as he scanned the train. He locked gaze with Dig through the doorway. His eyes widened before he leapt forward and ran at them.

The train picked up pace with a couple of strong jerks. Dig rose to a standing position. Jules whimpered behind him.

Shiv ran into view and grabbed the door railing, his shoes slapping along the platform as he tried to pull himself inside.

Dig leaned back and kicked. His foot thumped into Shiv's arm and broke his grasp. Shiv momentarily disappeared into the wake of the doorway then sprinted back into view to reach for the railing again.

Dig kicked a second time, his foot thumping into Shiv's chest—but this time Shiv held firm to the rail with clenched teeth and eyes like pinpricks.

Chook dragged himself up to stand beside Dig, his good hand holding the corridor wall for balance. He nodded at Dig and they kicked together this time, their feet thumping into Shiv's midriff.

Shiv winced and let go, but as he dropped he hooked two hands around Chook's ankle. Chook tried to kick him away but Shiv held tight, his feet scraping along the platform behind the train. Chook called out as he was dragged through the doorway, and Dig scrambled to grab hold of his good hand. Chook grimaced and held his grasp with a bulging forearm; his forehead was creased in fear.

"No!" Jules shouted, and tried to grab a handful of Chook's shirt. Together they strained to pull him back in the carriage—but Shiv's weight anchored him back.

The carriage accelerated toward the end of the platform where a metal fence bordered the drop to the tracks. The gap between the train and the fence was minimal, and threatened to guillotine Chook's waist.

Dig yanked again to no avail. Chook glanced ahead to the approaching fence, his long hair blowing across his face in the slipstream, then turned back to meet his sister's gaze. With a final furrow of his eyebrows he released his grip. His hand slipped out of Dig's sweaty grasp and he fell.

"No!" Jules screamed, her face contorted. She pushed to the doorway as the end of the platform ran away to be replaced by a blur of steep rocky embankment.

Dig leaned out behind her. Chook tumbled across the platform and collapsed in a static heap. Behind him, Shiv pushed himself up to his knees as the thugs arrived and hooked their hands under Chook's armpits.

"We've got to help him." Jules shouted, and glanced down to the rocky ground speeding past.

Dig put a hand on her shoulder. "You can't jump. It's too late. You'll break your legs." She gave him a pained look then stared back at the platform as it receded into the distance.

Finally she dropped to her rear in the train doorway, hooked her hands into the inside of her knees and curled up with her eyes clenched. Her shoulders hitched in sobs.

Crap, Dig thought. He squatted beside Jules and watched the passing scenery run away at an ever increasing speed. *We're in it deep now.*

13

JULES' SOBS EVENTUALLY DROPPED away, and she turned to lean back on the wall of the train corridor. Wet tracks ran down her cheeks.

"We need to go back and help him," she repeated.

Dig pursed his lips. "We'll help him somehow. But right now we're stuck on this train until the next stop."

"We can stop the train."

"And do what? Head straight back to the bar? We'll be massacred."

Jules' head dropped. "The next stop is miles away. It'll be too late."

"I think it's *already* too late. We don't even know where they took him." Dig bit at his nails. "Should we call the police?"

"Not the Goa police. They're on the Banyan payroll. They come into the brewhouse every month to pick up their payoffs." Her eyes were sullen and shoulders slumped. "There must be something we can do." She sat for a few minutes, staring out to the horizon.

Eventually Dig extended his hand. "Look. We'll get off at the next stop, and then we can work something out. But for now, let's go sit down."

She glanced at his hand, then up to meet his gaze. After a long pause, she reached out and Dig pulled her to her feet.

They moved into the humidity of the train carriage, ducking their heads to avoid a scalping on the low door frame. Passengers crowded into square wooden seats, sitting shoulder-to-shoulder, their brows lined with sweat, their children curled at their feet. The scent of body odour and something like mothballs filled the air. A stack of metal cages constricted the aisle, filled with chickens that beat the air with their wings as they passed. A boy lay on the ground with his head propped against one coop, sleeping. Dig stepped over him, then found a seat near a sleeping man wearing a turban and a long beard; he had a transparent plastic bag clutched to his chest, filled with documents. Dig lowered himself into the opposite seat. Jules sat beside the window and let her head rest on the frame.

"You okay?" Dig said.

She shrugged and stared out the window. "It's my fault," she said. "We should have left Goa a long time ago."

"There's no point blaming anyone. We just have to figure out what to do."

"Yes, but Chook was in my ear for months. Telling me to get out of Goa. Telling me to go home. And I didn't listen." She bit at her lip. "But at the end of the day, it wasn't me who paid the price. It was him."

Dig rubbed at his neck. "So why did you stay?"

"Staying was bad...but going home was worse."

A boy walked through the train with a pot of chai balanced on his shoulder. Dig handed the boy a few coins and he poured out two measures into small cardboard cups. He passed one of them to Jules; she gave a small nod and took a sip.

"Trouble at home?" Dig said.

Jules' lips thinned. "I had a car accident, and the police want to lock me up for it."

"What happened?"

"Ran over my step dad. Put him in wheelchair."

"Man. That's pretty hectic."

She shrugged and blew on her chai. "He won't be beating on Mum again."

Dig raised his eyebrows.

"So I came to Goa. And for a while things were good. Nice beaches. Lots of friendly people and big nights out. Got caught up in the whole atmosphere. Then Shiv offered me a few shifts in the bar in exchange for free board and some spending money—and well, it was too easy to refuse."

"Mind if I ask how you ended up with him?"

Jules' eyebrows drew together. "He was different when I first met him...friendly...caring even. He used to make me dinner. Maybe I didn't think it through at the time, but he helped me through a pretty tough stage. But the longer I stayed, the harder it was to leave. Before I knew it, I was part of the whole business and getting into the...extras."

"The opium in that place seemed pretty rampant."

She blinked. "I mostly had it under control. But yeah, with the amount of free stuff floating around it was hard not to get involved." She placed her elbows on her knees, and leaned forward with her chai cupped in her hands. "But once Max found out we were together she lost it. Told him he was putting the whole business at risk. Threatened to cut him out. He changed after that—resented me or something. Didn't trust me around other guys. Started getting violent." She stared out the window. Wide fields of rice and maize ran out to the horizon in rows, dotted with farmers driving bull ploughs through the earth. Jules sighed. "Chook figured out I was struggling and came over to get me. Wanted me to go home and face up to things. Get the family back together. But it wasn't that easy. I wasn't ready to deal with it. So...I blocked it all out, and pretended it would get better." She took a sip of chai, then shook her head and stared at her cup for a long moment before looking up. "What was your argument with Max about anyway?"

Dig explained everything that had happened over the last week. The funeral, Shiv's visit to Sydney, and then his efforts to track down Max. Jules listened, and as the story progressed she frowned.

"Why would they bother exporting them? Seems pretty risky."

Dig shrugged. "More money I guess."

"That doesn't sound like Max. She wouldn't trust just anyone with those hops."

"Well we used to get regular deliveries. The hops were used for our most popular beer." He scratched at his face. "But all that opium bioengineering stuff...it doesn't make sense. I know for a fact our beer back in Oz wasn't as potent as the stuff back there in the brewhouse. It tasted the same...but at the end of the day it was just a normal beer."

"There wouldn't have been enough in there for you to notice."

Dig looked at her blankly.

Jules sighed. "They produce two types of beer at the Banyan. One is the raw material, the unrefined, strong stuff they only sell under the table at the brewhouse. With the normal batches they sell commercially, they extract almost all the opiate during the brewing process until it scrapes under the relevant regulations."

Dig nodded. "Packages," he said under his breath.

"What?"

"Packages," Dig repeated. "That's what Dad was doing back home. Extracting the opiate during brewing and passing it back to Shiv in packages for distribution."

Jules nodded and pulled back her hair, exposing a slender neck and earrings made of small white shells. "I bet your beer was popular too, like the refined version of Banyan Bitter."

Dig frowned. "It was very popular. It was becoming the biggest selling Pale Ale in Australia."

"That's understandable. With all that trace opiate still in it."

"But that can't be legal?"

"Don't you get it? As long as it's below the legal limit it is. It's the same principle that some big cola companies use."

Dig furrowed his brow. "Huh?"

"Cola," Jules repeated. "They still use coca leaf extract as part of their recipe...the same type of leaf that cocaine's produced from."

"That's got to be bullshit."

"It's not. The cocaine gets extracted from the leaf until it gets below the regulatory limit—but the flavour's still there."

"That's nuts."

Jules shrugged. "That's common knowledge."

"What about Banyan Bitter then?"

"Even worse," Jules said. "The trace opiates in the beer trigger subtle cravings for every person who's ever had opiate based products in their lives—and that's not just for drugs like opium and heroin, it also applies to people who have taken things like codeine, an addictive drug found in over the counter pain medicine."

"But that's pretty much everyone."

"Exactly."

Dig shook his head. "So that's why the beers are so popular. The flavours tap into opiate cravings."

Jules nodded. "And that's why Max is so keen to keep it a secret."

Dig blinked rapidly. "We're totally stuffed here aren't we?"

"For sure."

"They aren't going to let us walk away from here."

"No chance."

"What the hell are we going to do?"

"I don't know." Jules rummaged through her pack. "But we need to get off this train. They know we're on it."

"Big time."

The man in the seat opposite them had woken up and was now eating yellow rice from a plastic bowl. Across the aisle, an elderly couple sat together. Their possessions were balled between them in a faded blanket. Through the window behind them a mountain range tracked past a gloomy sky, and a multi-coloured bird floated through the air.

The brakes squealed and the train began to slow. Jules straightened and leaned out the window. Her forehead furrowed. "The next stop's coming."

Dig nodded.

14

THE TRAIN CRUISED INTO THE STATION and shuddered to a stop with a hiss. As they rose from their seats, Dig glanced through the window to check the platform. People crowded against the doors of the train. Men dragged bags across the platform tiles and women hoisted children onto their hips.

Dig looked past the crowds to the station building behind, and his eyes caught on a group of figures standing against the weathered brick wall. One of the men scanned the crowd. Dig's stomach fell when he recognised him. It was Shiv, wearing a dour expression.

Dig dropped to a squat and shook Jules by the wrist. "He's here again!"

"Shiv?"

"Outside!"

She looked out the window, grimaced, and ducked down beside Dig. "Damn it."

"We can't get off. Let's just see what he does."

They sat on their heels inside the passage of the train, keeping out of sight. Passengers crowded past them through the aisle, pulling luggage. Vendors holding trays of samosas followed behind.

Eventually a whistle blew—long and loud, and Dig snuck a glance above the sill. Shiv looked up and down the platform. Suddenly, the train gave a jerk forward and began to accelerate. Shiv nodded to the thugs beside him, and the three men jogged toward the head of the train.

"I think they're going to get on."

"Where?"

"A couple of carriages up."

Jules bit at her lip. "We've got to get off."

They scampered through the carriage toward the rear exit, keeping low—but by the time they reached the doorway the end of the platform had dropped away to a blur of ballast and concrete. "Too late," Dig said.

Jules pressed her palm against her forehead. "Shit." Her chest rose and fell rapidly.

"Come on. We need to hide."

They hurried through the carriage toward the back of the train. As they moved, Dig scanned the carriage for a place to take cover, but there was nothing. The seats remained full of people, the baggage areas were jammed with luggage.

At the start of the next carriage, a side door revealed a toilet—dank and dirty and smelling like an open sewer. It was a small space, with barely enough room to squat over a shit-streaked hole in the floor. Above it, a cracked mirror hung above a murky metal sink. Dig glanced at Jules. She grimaced, put the back of her hand to her nose, and shook her head. They continued on.

The seats in the next carriage were also full, and they moved through quickly, casting furtive glances over their shoulders. At the end of the second carriage, their path was blocked by a closed metal door, marked with a sign that read *Guard Compartment*. A steel garbage bin was fixed to the wall beside the door, full of crumpled newspapers and plastic drink containers.

"That's it." Jules' eyes were wide. "No more carriages."

Dig swore, then looked around him. "You smoke right?"

"Yes," she said in a strained voice.

"Give me your lighter."

Her brow furrowed before she unzipped a pocket in her skirt and handed it to him.

"I'll be back in a sec." Dig sifted through the garbage bin beside the door and extracted some newspapers and drink containers. He then ran back through the passenger cabin.

When he reached the toilet, he dropped the newspapers to his feet and began ripping the pages away, rolling them up into crude balls and throwing them onto the floor. He continued until he had covered the cubicle in paper. He placed the empty plastic water bottles on the centre of the pile, and with a shaking hand he knelt down and held the lighter to the bottom of the heap in several places.

The flames flickered small at first, then climbed and spread throughout the pile. As the heat intensified, Dig pulled the door to the toilet closed. He peered into the next carriage and sucked in his breath as three men entered. Shiv had arrived.

Dig ran back down the aisle to where Jules was standing at the end of the train with her hands on her hips. "What's going on?" she hissed.

"Shiv's coming. Next carriage." He reached out to the Guard Compartment door and rapped on the metal.

He waited a few moments, then pounded again, the force biting into the point of his knuckles. "Come on..." he said under his breath, and glanced back over his shoulder.

The handle turned and the door creaked open enough for a man in a faded blue shirt and peaked black cap to ease his head through the gap. "Yes?"

"Hey. There's a fire in the toilet of the next carriage. There's smoke coming out from under the door."

The man looked at him blankly. "In the toilet?"

"Yes. You should hurry!" He turned and pointed into the carriage— now filled with the brown haze of burnt plastic.

The man opened the door and squinted further down the train. Strained voices now echoed down the aisle. He nodded, adjusted his hat, and hurried into the carriage.

Before the door to the guard's compartment swung closed, Dig threw his foot out to catch it between the door and the frame. He glanced behind him, but the guard was already halfway down the coach.

Dig pried the door open. "Come on." Jules followed him in, and he pulled the door shut with a click.

The guard's compartment was a small room with a desk in front of a rear facing window. The room stunk like stale cigarette smoke, and was flanked by open doorways on both walls with only links of chain separating the compartment from the speeding ballast below. A chipped speaker hung from the ceiling. Behind the train, the tracks ran away at a rapid pace.

The train bounced to the left, and Dig put a hand out to steady himself. "Looks like we're stuck in here for now."

Jules fingered her necklace, then sat on the floor with her back to the door. "I can't believe they got here so fast. They must have sped from Goa."

Dig pressed his ear against the door, listening. All he could hear was the clackety-clack of the wheels below. The smell of burning plastic intensified, and a plume of brown smoke choked the air behind the train.

Jules pointed to the base of the door, where a sliver of light beamed through the gap between it and the floor. A shadow materialised in the light. They held their breath.

Rap Rap Rap!

They jumped. The sound seemed to come from all around them. Dig put a finger to his lips.

They waited.

The door handle turned and the lock caught. Dig swallowed and held tightly to the desk beside him as the train jostled along the tracks. Jules hugged her knees on the floor.

Rap Rap Rap!

And silence. The stench of the smoke was acrid and more pronounced now, filling the room. Dig could taste it at the back of his throat.

"Hello?" It was a deep voice, muffled through the door. "Anyone in there?"

It was Shiv.

"Jules?"

Jules dropped her head to her chest and closed her eyes; she was shaking. Dig surveyed the room for some sort of weapon. A wrench, or even a broom would do. But the room was empty. There was nothing.

"You need to open the door Jules. We know you're in there. The guard said he saw you in this carriage."

Jules laced her fingers around the back of her head.

"We have your brother. He's hurt, so we sent him back to Hampi to...take care of him. If you want to see him...then you need to come with us now. Otherwise, in a couple of days he'll be chopped up and fed to the crocodiles." Jules turned to look at the closed door. Her forehead furrowed and a tear welled in the corner of her eye.

There was a pause. "We know you took the money from the house. If you give it back now, we can try to figure things out."

Jules pursed her lips.

"And as for your friend Dig, he needs to come too. If he doesn't, in a couple of days' time I'm taking a return trip to Australia to see which one of his mother's ears she wants to keep." Dig clenched his fist and tapped it against his lips.

"So open the door...*now*. And come with us. We just need to talk."

Jules glanced at Dig, and he shook his head. She stared forlornly at the door, then pushed herself to her feet. She brought a shaking hand to her lip, then reached for the handle. Dig grabbed her wrist, his eyes wide.

The speaker above their head gave a whine of feedback and then crackled into life; a warbled voice then echoed across the line. *'Fire! Fire! In carriage seven! Stop the train...stop the train!'*

A loud squeal of metal-on-metal drilled into Dig's ears and they were thrown forward. Dig's head cracked hard against a metal bulkhead. Jules fell to her rear. The clackety-clack slowed its tempo beneath them and the smell of burning brake pads filled the air. With a final whine, the train ground to a shuddering stop, and they both slid across the floor, crashing into the rear table. A drawer popped out and fell to the ground, spilling out a handful of timetables and a magazine with a cover of a busty, dark haired woman wearing nothing but a suggestive pout.

It was eerily quiet, save for the hissing of gas escaping from somewhere below them. Behind the closed door, Dig could hear Shiv and his offsiders swearing and complaining.

"Let's go," Dig whispered and crawled along the floor to the exterior ladder. He unhooked the chain link and began lowering himself backwards out the door when he glanced back at Jules. She lay back on one elbow with a vacant stare. Dig reached up and tugged her ankle. "Come on!"

She nodded, and followed him out the door.

Dig stepped down the ladder and lowered himself to the earth. His foot landed on something slippery and slid out from under him, dropping him to his knees. His hand went to the ground, and groped something slimy and wet. A foul stench was in the air—the stench of human waste. Dig held his breath and looked around him.

Further up the tracks, an elderly man wearing dirty pants and a grimy collared shirt was squatting, relieving himself. He glanced at Dig with a passive nonchalance as he deposited the contents of his bowels beside the track. Dig stared at his own hand, and realised it was covered in excrement. In fact, the ground around him was dotted with brown patches.

Rudimentary shacks ran parallel with the now stationary train, each constructed of corrugated iron panels, blue plastic sheeting, and cardboard. A grubby boy emerged from the passageways between the shacks, unzipped his pants and relieved himself further up the track.

"What the..." Dig said.

"Slum toilet." Jules climbed down the ladder beside him. "Come on." She ran away toward the shacks. Dig wiped his hand against a rail and followed her.

"Hey!" The voice came from the train. Shiv leaned out of the doorway to the main carriage. "Jules!"

Jules skipped across the track ballast before disappearing into a dark alleyway between the buildings. Dig covered the distance in long strides and followed her into the passage.

Shadowy dwellings of corrugated iron lined up on both sides of the corridor, with small children sitting in the doorways. Dig skipped between muddy puddles on the ground; the stink of urine filled the air.

Jules dodged left into a shadowy passageway, barely shoulder width, that ran away between two high mudbrick walls. As Dig followed her around the corner, he glanced back to see Shiv and the thugs pushing into the corridor. They were catching up.

They ran through the passage, ducking below a clothesline while their shoes slapped against the muddy ground. A mangy dog appeared from a doorway and snapped at Dig's heels.

The passage rose up a set of stairs, then opened out into an enclosed courtyard surrounded by tall, mudbrick buildings with darkened doorways. A boy knelt in the centre of the courtyard, pumping water from a well. Jules stopped, her chest heaving, and turned to Dig with wide eyes. "We're trapped."

Footsteps echoed behind them, and Dig's stomach clenched. "Come on," he said, and ran past the boy into the nearest door.

The room was small and dark, and smelt like smoke and mud. It took a moment for his eyes to adjust. A table stood in the centre of the room, supporting a stack of plates. Against the back wall, a ladder led up through the ceiling. Dig ran to it and climbed. Voices shouted from the doorway behind them.

In the upper level, the ceiling was low and Dig's knees popped as he scurried across the room. A mattress lay in one corner, and light streamed through a solitary window. He pushed his head through the window frame to see a tangled sea of roofs spread out ahead of him, split by the top of a fragmented mud wall that zigzagged between the buildings like a broken path.

Jules appeared in the window beside him.

"The wall," Dig said. "Outside." He helped her out through the window opening. The sleeve of her shirt tore on the frame as she passed through.

Dig climbed out behind her and lowered himself to the top of the wall. It was a couple of hand spans wide, but the bricks were jagged and wobbly. The mortar between the blocks was flaking away.

A voice echoed above them. Dig glanced up, then turned to Jules. "Go," he said. "Along the wall, I'll catch up."

"What are you doing?"

"Trying to stop them."

Jules frowned, then turned and began to walk along the top of the wall with her hands spread wide for balance. Each side dropped down to the roofs below.

Dig pulled his pack to his chest and unzipped the front pocket. He fished out his house keys and began prising at the mortar between the bricks. After a moment the first brick split away from the top of the wall.

He extracted it, then balanced it precariously back in position. He copied this action with the three adjacent bricks before pushing to his feet.

Above him, Shiv's head shot out through the window frame. "Here!" Shiv shouted behind him, and began to climb out through the window.

Dig turned and walked along the wall, as fast as he dared, trying to keep his focus on his feet. Sweat dripped down his temples. A breeze pushed at his side and tried to send him over the edge.

Dig glanced backwards to see Shiv drop down to the wall. His foot came down on a loose brick and it fell away; his arms pinwheeled and he overbalanced, dropping over the side.

Shiv hit the roof of one of the shacks, taking the impact on his shoulder. It imploded around him, and he dropped down through the building. Pieces of the ceiling followed him down in a cloud of billowing dust.

Dig turned his attention forward again, moving along the wall as fast as he dared. Jules stood motionless ahead of him. As he caught up he saw she was staring down at a pile of dirty plastic rubbish heaped against a wall on a street.

"Jump?"

"Yep."

Jules dropped first, punching into the pile of garbage to her waist. Dig landed beside her, and they pushed out of the trash to the street edge. Motor rickshaws moved along the street in two directions, bouncing through potholes and spewing exhaust behind them. Streams of brown liquid ran down the gutters.

Dig waved at a motor rickshaw and it rumbled to a stop beside them. They jumped in the back. "Just get us out of here! As quick as you can."

The driver wobbled his head and the machine moved forward.

Dig peered behind them. The rickshaw trundled slowly up the street, but Shiv was nowhere to be seen amongst the crowds. He hunched down in his seat and willed the driver onward.

When the rickshaw reached the end of the dirt road it turned onto a stretch of asphalt. The driver pulled back the throttle, and the wind blew through their hair as fields of rice and grain appeared on both sides of the street. Piles of rubbish burnt on the fence line. Dig watched the road behind them for a few minutes before turning back to Jules. "I think we lost them."

Jules pursed her lips and gave a small shrug. "Along with my only chance to see my brother."

"You couldn't go with them. They'd chop you up."

"I need to help him."

"We will," Dig said with a deep breath. "I know where he is."

"Where?"

"Shiv said he took Chook to Hampi. I was there yesterday...in their brewery. I can take you there."

"Okay, let's go then."

Dig frowned. "We can't just turn up, knock on the front door and ask for him back."

"Well what else can we do?"

"I don't know." He scratched his head. "Maybe we should just lay low for a bit and figure out a plan."

Jules sighed and turned to look out the window. The sun was dropping behind the passing fields. "We'll head to Badami for the night. It's a quiet town that's close to Hampi. They won't think to look there."

"Fine. That'll give me time to think. There are just...some parts of this that still don't make sense."

"Like what?"

"Like how the hell my father got caught up in this in the first place, and why he let it go on for so long when it seemed like he didn't want to be part of it."

Jules leaned forward to the driver. "Can you take us to Badami please?"

"Badami?" The driver's eyes widened. "This is very long way."

"Yeah, I know."

"Going to be an expensive rickshaw ride," Dig muttered.

"Don't worry. I just came into a bit of cash."

Dig raised his eyebrows. "How much did you steal from the house?"

"A few million rupee. Straight out of Shiv's private safe."

"How much is that in dollars?"

"I don't know...about sixty grand?"

"You're off the Christmas card list."

Jules nodded and gave a weak smile. She moved closer to Dig and rested her head back against the seat. Dig's stomach gave a flutter as he felt the warmth of her skin against his forearm.

Outside, the broken asphalt ran away below the rickshaw. The motor hummed in their ears as they bounced along the road. The sun dropped away to a steamy night, and the scenery outside became a blur of streetlights and lit shopfronts.

15

"EXCUSE ME SIR..." The voice crept into Dig's dreams; he became aware of a silence around him. "Hello please."

He opened his eyes. The driver watched him through the rear view mirror. The dimly lit rectangle of a doorway stood in the darkness of the roadside. He checked his watch; it was 2 a.m. They had been driving for eight hours.

"Badami sir."

Dig glanced down at Jules. She lay back against the seat with her eyes closed, mouth slightly ajar and head resting against his shoulder. A small smattering of freckles covered her nose.

He bumped her with an elbow and she stirred, then opened her eyes and stretched. "We're here?"

Dig nodded.

Jules turned to the driver. "Is this a hotel?"

"Yes. Badami Hotel."

Jules paid him, and they climbed stiffly out of the rickshaw.

As they entered their room, Jules dropped her bag to the bed and headed for the shower. Dig rubbed at his eyes and walked out to a balcony.

The hotel sat on the edge of a wide lake framed by cliffs on both sides. A full moon reflected in the water's mirrored surface. At the far side of the lake the outline of a temple bordered the shore, and below him water lapped against a stepped sandstone ghat. The air was warm and still, and Dig took a long breath in through his nose.

After a while, Dig glanced back inside to see Jules rummaging through her bag. Her hair was wet, and she was wrapped only in a towel. She looked up and caught Dig's gaze, then raised an eyebrow. "You want a shower?"

"Oh, yeah...I do." He found a towel and a bar of soap, and headed into the bathroom. The hot water drummed into his head. It was a relief to be able to scrub away the grime of the last two days.

When he returned to the room Jules was sitting on the balcony. She leaned back and the smoke from her cigarette wafted up around her.

"Great view huh?"

Jules nodded, then took another drag on her cigarette. The smoke smelled sweet and musky. Dig sat beside her and leaned back with his feet on the balcony railing.

"When do we get my brother?" Jules said.

Dig fiddled with the seam of his shirt. "Tomorrow," he said, and sighed. "Know any armies for hire?"

Jules' expression was blank.

"That was a joke."

"Oh."

Dig shrugged. "Seriously though, we need to come up with something better than just walking in there."

Jules blew out another cloud of smoke. "Nuclear bomb," she said, then mimicked the sound of an explosion. "Boom! Everything gone." She stared vacantly out over the balcony.

Dig offered a strained smile, and glanced at the cigarette in her hand. "You okay?"

Jules rested the cigarette on an ashtray and pushed herself shakily to her feet. "Toilet." She walked back into the room.

Dig nodded, and watched her go. Her shoulder glanced off the door frame as she passed through, and she threw her arms out for balance. "Oops."

Dig studied the cigarette smouldering in the tray, then leaned over and picked it up gingerly with thumb and forefinger, and brought it to his nose. It smelled sweet and musky, yet pungent, and his temples tingled for a moment. He returned the cigarette to the ashtray, then leaned back with his hands behind his head, staring blankly out into the night.

He waited that way until the cigarette burnt three quarters down its length and extinguished itself. Dig frowned and looked back toward the bathroom. The door was open, but Jules was nowhere to be seen.

He found her lying on the bed. She was on her back, with her head tilted to one side and her eyes closed, wearing a white singlet top and brown cotton track pants. A fan revolved slowly above her head and blew her hair against the pillow. As he approached, he could hear her breathing in a slow, regular pattern.

"Jules?"

She remained on her back, unmoved, breathing deeply.

Dig frowned and walked back to the balcony. He returned to his seat and looked back out at the view, chewing at his lip.

Eventually the moon faded from the sky and the sun rose over the top of the cliffs. Dig watched it climb, unable to sleep. The streets came to life with dogs barking, motorbikes puttering through the streets and honking horns. His stomach grumbled.

He shuffled back into the room and stood beside the bed. Jules was now on her side, and tucked under the sheets.

"Jules? You awake?"

She stirred, rubbed at her eyes and gave a grunt. "What?"

"I'm going to grab some food. You want a coffee or something?"

She sat up in her bed and looked around the room with puffy eyes and a furrowed brow. "Yeah. Coffee is good," she croaked, and tucked her hair behind her ears as she stepped down to the floor. She walked out to the balcony with one arm wrapped across her ribs; goose bumps covered her arms.

Dig watched her go, then after a moment he followed her out. She stood staring at the view, holding the remains of last night's cigarette in a shaky hand. She lifted it to her lips and took a long drag before exhaling a cloud of smoke with the same sweet, musky odour from the night before, then gave a warped smile.

"Another day in paradise!" she giggled, and reached for the balcony railing before dropping heavily into the seat.

Dig scratched at the back of his neck. "You brought some gear with you then?"

"Just a few leftovers."

"Today? Is that a good idea?"

"Don't see why not." She arched an eyebrow. "It's probably my *last* day, so I may as well try to smooth it out a bit."

"Feels to me like you're giving up."

She glared at him. "Feels to me like giving up is the best way. We should just walk in there with our hands up and plead for forgiveness."

"No."

"Well what's your plan?"

Dig's body tensed and he put a hand to his hip. "Well maybe if you actually tried to help me, instead of spending your time in a drug-induced stupor, I might have one!"

"You do it your way. I'll do it mine."

Dig face flushed and he clenched his teeth. "I'm going for a walk. We'll leave at lunchtime." He paused. "And you should know, when I travelled into Hampi a few days ago they had roadblocks set up on the street, searching for drugs. So if you haven't ditched all your *leftovers* by then we'll both end up in jail and your brother will be sent to the bottom of the river."

Jules' brow creased and she turned away.

Dig left the building and followed the stepped concrete ghats around the side of the lake. Women sat on the water's edge, washing clothes and spreading them to dry on the concrete. Dirty pigs rooted through trash. The chirp of small birds flitted through the open air above him.

He purchased a bread roll and a banana at a small bakery. He pocketed the roll and bit into the banana as he moved down the street.

The street was lined with shopfronts, and vendors stood in the doorways. A woman from a souvenir store stepped out with a wooden elephant in her hand, nodding; a man with a long-haired moustache and turban tried to entice him into his tailor shop to get measured for a new suit; a small boy accosted him, determined to place a string bracelet on his wrist in exchange for money. But Dig refused them all. His mind churned. He needed space to think. He looked across to the empty cliffs that hugged the lake, and headed toward them.

By keeping the cliffs in view, he managed to navigate his way through a maze of tight alleyways behind the ghats, and reach the base of the mountain. As the road ended, a stone archway framed a set of stairs that zigzagged their way up the side of the hill. Dig began to climb.

The cobbled path snaked through large boulders, bushes and patches of orange dirt. Dig climbed the steps in a slow rhythm, his breath in time with his footfalls. Sweat matted the hairs on his forearms together and ran down his backbone.

After some time, the stairs levelled out to reveal the top of the hill. Here, an ancient rectangular building sat on the cliff edge, constructed from blocks of weathered red sandstone. A stone spire climbed to the sky at one end of the building, and a bird with green and blue feathers preened itself on the peak. A small metal sign at the front of the temple announced the structure was called the *Malegitti Shivalaya* temple.

A flat stone courtyard ran out to the edge of the cliff, ringed by a waist-high wall. The ground dropped away steeply on the other side, down to the lake below.

Dig hoisted himself onto the wall and dangled his legs over the drop. The sandstone was hot on the back of his thighs. A dry, dusty breeze blew past him and cooled the sweat on his arms and legs. He looked out at the view.

To his left, a waterfall cascaded over the top of the mountain and dropped down into the lake with a trickling whisper. On the opposite side of the lake, the dark shadows of caves cut into the red sandstone of the mountain. To the right, the concrete ghats dammed the lake and formed the edge of the town. Dig spotted their hotel, and an image of Jules came into his mind, sitting on the balcony, smoking. He clenched his teeth.

He took in a deep breath, and tried to think clearly. By the end of the day he needed to confront Maxine again, yet if they just walked straight into the brewery they were doomed. He was scared. But did he have any choice?

Could he just return home and hope for the best? He thought not. Now he understood the full workings of the Banyan Brewery, they weren't going to let him escape. He sighed and shifted in his seat, then reached into his pocket and retrieved the bread roll. He bit into it with a crunch.

A flapping approached from behind him, and Dig turned to see the multicoloured bird cruise down from the top of the temple and land beside him on the wall. It cocked its head.

Dig tucked the bread roll under his armpit and waved at the bird. "Shoo," he said, and the bird squawked, fell away over the cliff, then circled back around to perch on top of the temple spire.

Dig bit back into the bread roll, when from behind his right ear someone spoke.

"Don't push it away."

Dig flinched, and turned to an elderly man standing behind him. He had a bushy white beard and long grey hair that surrounded a wrinkled, weather-beaten face. A yellow circle of paint was positioned between his eyebrows. He wore a white robe and a length of yellow fabric draped around his shoulders.

He pointed at the wall beside Dig. "Mind if I sit?"

Dig looked him up and down, then shook his head. "No," he said, then after a pause, added: "But I'll just let you know upfront that I'm not interested in buying any type of blessing or statues or tours or photo opportunities or anything like that."

The man laughed. "No problem." He sat down. "I've nothing to sell."

Dig dipped his chin. "Sorry. They were a bit pushy down in the shops."

"Understandable." The man glanced back at the temple.

"This is a beautiful place," Dig offered.

"Shh," the man whispered. "Please, be quiet."

Dig followed the man's gaze back toward the temple. "Are you the priest here? In this temple?"

"Yes. Now do you want to see something amazing?"

Dig blinked. "Maybe."

"Then sit up straight. And still. Like me."

Dig took a glance behind him, expecting to see a boy hiding somewhere, ready to steal his wallet. But the courtyard was empty.

"Now wait, be still, and listen."

Dig frowned and scratched at his arm.

"Here it comes," the man said. "Do you hear it?"

Dig listened. He heard a distant rustle of the wind in the trees, and nothing else but the echo of the large, open space before him. "I don't think so."

"It's coming."

Then, Dig did hear something. The sound of wings pushing through the air.

"Don't move."

The flapping finished with a click of talons on stone. Again, the multicoloured bird sat beside him on the wall.

Dig frowned and tucked his bread roll back under his armpit.

"I said don't move."

"He wants my breakfast."

"He doesn't eat bread," the priest said, his eyes wide. "Can't you see?"

Dig shrugged. "See what?"

"This is a Rainbow Bee Eater."

Dig looked between the bird and the priest. He felt more confused than ever.

"They are extremely rare in India." the priest said. "To see one here is, well, completely irregular. In fact, I think they are from Australia."

Dig narrowed his eyes. "How do you know that?"

"Well, I'm a small-time priest, and big-time birdwatcher. That's why I took the position up here. There are hundreds of species living in these cliffs. But none of these guys. Not ever."

The bird took a few steps toward Dig, then stopped.

"So close!" the priest whispered, and grabbed Dig's arm. His fingernails dug into his skin.

Dig studied the animal. It was small, about the size of his palm, with green wings and a lower body of bright blue. Its head was a pale yellow, and a black stripe of feathers ran across its eyes. "I know these birds," Dig said. "I think they have a nest in the chimney of my home...in Australia."

"You see?"

Dig nodded, but something else nagged at him. He leaned in and studied the bird again. Then it hit him. It was the same species that distracted the driver as he hid on the truck travelling to the docks.

"And I saw one of these in Goa," he said, blinking rapidly. "And...in a tunnel in Hampi. It ate a hornet that was about to attack me."

"Aah yes." The priest's eyes lit up. "As the name suggests, they only eat insects...and bees and wasps in particular." He glanced at Dig. "But if you have seen it many times before, then that explains it."

"That explains what?"

"That explains where it came from."

"I didn't smuggle it over if that's what you mean."

The man smiled. "There is more to our world than our physical form. We all have connections with the world around us. Some stronger than others. You have a bond with this creature. Your auras are intertwined. I felt it when you first arrived."

Dig raised his eyebrows.

"You don't feel it?"

Dig shrugged and looked back down at the animal. "No." He scratched his arm. "But, even if I did, what does it mean?"

"That's for you to figure out. We Hindus believe in spiritual affinity with the animals. We also believe in Samsara, or reincarnation."

"Reincarnation?"

"Yes," the priest said. "Now please. Just relax for a moment."

Dig frowned and tried to sit still.

The bird turned its head, then slowly stepped forward along the wall until it was inches from Dig's leg. Dig expected it to take a peck at the bread roll tucked under his arm—but instead, its beak tugged twice at the pocket of his pants before the bird chirped loudly. It then turned and took flight, gliding out over the edge of the cliff and disappearing.

"Wow," the priest said, watching it go. "Just amazing." He nodded slowly. "This really is a special day."

Dig pursed his lips.

"Don't you agree? Aren't you happy to be part of that?"

Dig gave a weak smile. "Yeah, sure."

The man looked up at the sky, took a deep breath, and let it out again. "So what brings you to India?"

Dig paused. "I came here to sort out a...family issue."

"Okay. And have you had success?"

"No. It's not looking good at the moment."

"Well maybe this should be a lesson. We all face challenges at some point in our lives. To arrest it, you need to get out of your head and be more aware of the world around you." He reached over and tapped his finger on Dig's temple.

Dig ducked away and smiled. He looked in the sky for the bird, but it was gone.

He thought about the animal tugging at his shorts. After a moment, he reached into the pocket and emptied the contents out to the wall. A handful of coins spilled out with a remnant of dried sausage, and a folded, wrinkled piece of paper.

He lifted the paper and opened it out to press it flat on the top of the wall. It was the Banyan invoice.

He studied the invoice closely. He understood most parts of it—such as the description of the hops and the bank details, but there were a couple of parts that confused him.

INVOICE

Banyan Breweries
Hampi 583227
PO Box 5089
(+91) 09 242 641559

Invoice No.	72435
Date:	7th Sept
Due Date:	7th Oct

Description	Amount
50 kg Dried Hops	$2,000
50 kg Dried Hops	$2,000
50 kg Dried Hops	$2,000
50 kg Dried Hops	$2,000
50 kg Dried Hops	$2,000
Customs Shabdkosh	$2,350
Bay-Ta Brewing Yeast	$5,000
Net Amount Due:	**$17,350**

Preferred Payment Method - Direct Bank Transfer
Bank: Canara Bank
Branch: Hampi
IFCS Code: CNRB0001187
Account: 0154563

He held the invoice out to the priest. "Do you know what this means?" he said. "Customs Shabdkosh?"

"Shabdkosh means tax in Hindi. So that would be a customs tax."

Dig nodded slowly. He then looked down at the final payment item on the invoice—the mystifying *Bay-ta Brewer's Yeast* that he had never seen delivered in Australia.

"And this word? *Bay-ta*?"

The man turned down his lips. "Bay-ta means son."

"Sun? As in up in the sky?"

"No," the man said. "As in father and son."

Dig felt a quickening in his chest. "So this is a *son* payment?"

The man leaned forward and looked at the paper. "It looks like it."

Dig's eyes widened and he stared out over the lake. "This is...crazy."

He sat there for a few minutes, staring at the horizon, before he turned back to the priest. "I've got it."

But the priest was gone, and the courtyard was empty.

Dig's brow furrowed. "Did he just...disappear?"

"No," shouted a voice, and the priest's head leant around the courtyard wall. "I'm just taking a piss."

Dig pushed himself to his feet. "I think I need to go now."

"Okay. Then good luck with your family issues. But remember, get out of your head, and be aware of your surroundings. And watch out for your beautiful friend."

Dig nodded, then turned to jog back down the hill.

The sun was blazing in the middle of the sky when he returned to the hotel. Jules sat on the balcony, her legs resting on the railing. She wore a shirt with green flowers imprinted on it. Her eyes were sullen.

"Hey there."

Jules turned, then looked back at the view. "Hey."

"I brought you a coffee and some bananas."

"Thanks." She took them from him. "Where did you go?"

"I just needed to walk. I had lots to think about. You okay?"

She shrugged.

Dig ran a hand through his hair. "Well maybe I can cheer you up," he said with butterflies dancing in his stomach. "As I might have figured some things out."

"What do you mean?"

Dig handed her the Banyan invoice.

"What's this?"

"An invoice from the Banyan Brewery. To our company back in Australia." He pointed to it. "Look at this payment—for *Bay-ta Brewer's Yeast.*"

Jules' face was blank.

"We've never been delivered any yeast from Banyan. They only sent us hops. Which got me thinking about this *Bay-ta* bit."

"Bay-ta? Doesn't that mean—"

"Son," Dig said, nodding quickly. "I'm thinking it was some type of veiled payment for a son, like, you know, maintenance or something...for Maxine's son."

"She has a son?"

"I met him in Hampi. His name was Raj. And she has a husband too...Girish is his name. But I don't think Girish is Raj's father." He swallowed. "I think it might have been my dad."

"But that would make that Raj boy your—"

"Half-brother."

Jules' eyes narrowed. "You sure you aren't overreacting here?"

"I don't think so. Remember back at the bar? Maxine said something about me coming over here to *break up her family*. Now I understand why she said it. She thought I knew."

"Well that would explain why Maxine was exporting the hops to your dad. It did seem strange."

Dig blinked. "I didn't think of that."

"And it would also explain why she pulled the deal as soon as your dad died."

"You're right!" Dig paced around the room, nodding. "This is...great! If Dad was receiving the hops as a way to disguise some type of secret maintenance payment, then maybe we have a chance!"

Jules' eyebrows knitted together.

"It's time to go to Hampi. And I'm going to tell Maxine if she doesn't leave all of us alone then I'm going to let out her precious secret."

"Are you sure this is right?"

Dig took a deep breath. "No. But at the same time, it's the best we've got."

"And if you're wrong? Or she doesn't care?"

"Then we're toast." Dig picked up his pack. "But I'm going for it. You ready?"

She bit her lip, and nodded.

They left the building and walked down the main shopping street, looking for a taxi. As they passed the tailor, the man with the turban waved from the doorway, smiling. "Have a good trip Jules!" Jules gave him a quick wave and dropped her head.

"You know him?"

"I got him to make me this shirt this morning. I ripped my other one when we ran from the train."

Dig smiled. "You should have told me you were going. I'm low on clean undies. He could have whipped me up a few."

"Green flowery ones as well?"

"Of course."

They found a taxi at the end of the street, and settled into the back seat. The car threaded through the alleys at the base of the cliffs before pulling out onto the open road. Dig glanced at the top of the cliff as he passed.

"Do you know much about Hindus?" he said. "You know, religion wise?"

"A bit. Why?"

"I met a Hindu priest up on the cliff this morning who was screwing with my mind. Talking about stuff like spiritual connections and reincarnation."

Jules' eyes narrowed. "I don't know about reincarnation. But I believe a person's spirit still hangs around after they die."

"In what way?"

She picked at her skirt. "A close friend of mine died last year. And it wasn't until she was gone that I realised the important place she had in my life, and the spirit that left with her. I realised I took our relationship a bit for granted, you know?" She gave a small shrug, then met Dig's gaze. Bags hung below her eyes. "But then I realised she wasn't totally gone. She still popped up in my mind now and then...at the weirdest times. I could feel her. It was like her spirit came to visit—the same as when she was alive." She sighed. "So these days, when I think of her, it makes me more happy than sad. Because I know she hasn't totally gone, and I know that she's still looking out for me."

Dig stared out the window. A small tingling rush crept up the back of his neck, and he fought back tears that built in the corners of his eyes.

"You father only just died right?" Jules said. "Give it some time, and you might start to feel him turn up in everyday life. You just have to keep your eyes open."

Dig shrugged and gave her a weak smile.

16

AS THE TAXI APPROACHED HAMPI the nerves ramped up in Dig's stomach and he bit his fingernails ragged. Jules hugged her knees to her chest.

"Excuse me driver," she said in a wavering voice. "Can you stop for a toilet break soon?"

The driver nodded, and a short time later they turned off the road into an ancient petrol station with two rusted pumps standing in a weed-covered forecourt. The driver killed the engine and began to fill up.

Jules retrieved her bag and stepped out to the tarmac. "Won't be long."

Dig nodded, drumming his fingers on the seat as he watched her walk toward the rear of the building.

Beside him, the pump sloshed out petrol in a steady stream, and the numbers ticked over at pace. Eventually, the machine clicked off and the driver returned the nozzle to its cradle, walked inside to pay, and returned to the car.

As the engine started, Dig hung his head outside the window, looking left and right, but Jules was nowhere to be seen. He muttered under his breath, then leaned forward. "I'll be back in a minute." The driver wobbled his head.

Dig walked across the station forecourt and around the back of the building. Behind it, a rectangle of gravel flanked the rear brick wall.

Jules stood at the far end of the clearing, holding a cigarette and staring into the distance. The smoke wafted toward Dig, filling his nostrils with the same sweet, musky odour from back at the hotel. He scowled as he approached. "The taxi's waiting."

Jules turned quickly, startled. She dropped the cigarette to the ground and stamped it out. "Coming now." She exhaled two long streams of smoke from her nostrils, then looked to the ground and turned in a circle. "Where's my pack?"

"On your back."

"Oh!" She grinned. "Silly me." She stumbled toward the car.

Dig strode ahead of her and cut off her path.

She frowned. "That was the last of it okay! It's all gone. So don't freak out."

"You sure? The roadblock's probably just around the corner."

"Yes! You're worse than my bloody brother." She moved to step around him, but Dig blocked her path again. She took a deep breath, then held her pack out. "Do you want me to empty it out for you? I'll do it!"

Dig met her gaze for a few seconds, then stepped aside.

"Come on," she said. "Let's go do this." She trudged back to the taxi.

They drove through the early afternoon as they approached the outskirts of Hampi. Jules rested her head on the window frame, eyes closed. Dig stared out the front windscreen and fidgeted with the zip on his pack. The rock formations of the Hampi region appeared on the horizon.

As the vehicle topped a rise, Dig recognised a cluster of road barriers blocking the road. A thin-faced policeman stood behind them, waving a fluorescent stick to the shoulder.

Dig elbowed Jules, and her eyes popped open. "Police check." She nodded and rubbed at her eyes.

The taxi slowed, rumbled into the road shoulder, and stopped. The policeman lowered his head through the window frame and studied them, then gestured for them to get out.

Dig stepped down to the gravel with his bag. Jules stood beside him with tight shoulders and her arms folded.

The thin policeman walked to a hut beside the road barriers and spoke a few words, and a heavyset policeman with a thick, grey moustache and peaked cap appeared in the doorway. Dig recognised him as the police chief from his visit through the checkpoint a few days before.

The chief glanced at the pair, then hitched up his pants and trudged toward them.

He stopped in front of Dig and looked him over, then spoke to the taxi driver. The taxi driver popped the boot of the car, and the thin policeman produced a heavy torch and shone it through the space, lifting up the carpet and searching through the spare wheel.

The chief turned to Dig and picked at his teeth with a toothpick. "I've seen you before."

Dig nodded. "I was here a few days ago."

"Why have you come back?"

Dig glanced at Jules. "I wanted to show Hampi to my friend. It's a beautiful place."

The man pointed to a table beside them. "Open your bag."

Dig dumped his bag down and pulled it open. The policeman rummaged through it, pulling items out and placing them on the surface. He studied the items for a moment. "Okay," he said before turning his attention to Jules. "Your bag please."

Jules lifted her bag and placed it on the tabletop with a shaking hand.

The policeman began to sift through it. "First time in Hampi?" he said.

"Yes," Jules said quietly.

The policeman extracted the contents, lining them up onto the table. Jules stood with her hands clasped together at her waist. Her face was ashen.

Once the bag was empty, the policemen picked it up and shook it, then chewed on his toothpick and watched her. "Why are you so nervous?"

Jules blinked. "I...I don't know." Her gaze dropped.

The policeman glanced from Dig to Jules with narrow eyes, then gave a small nod and turned to shuffle back toward the roadside hut.

The thin policeman waved them away. "You can go."

Jules herded her possessions into her pack, and they returned to the back seat of the taxi. The driver started the car and directed it through the barriers to the open road, moving up through the gears toward Hampi.

Dig turned to Jules. "Everything alright?"

Jules shot him a glassy stare. "Fine." She turned to look back out the window. The tag from her shirt protruded against her neck.

Dig watched her for a moment, then turned his gaze forward again. Buildings appeared on both sides of the road. They were nearly in town.

17

THE TAXI PULLED TO A STOP on the Hampi bazaar, and they stepped out to the road and paid the driver through the open window. The street was busy, and people milled around the stalls that lined the edge of the dirt road. A man roasted nuts over a bucket of charcoal, and the tangy smoke wafted into their faces. A large white cow with sagging jowls sat in the middle of the thoroughfare and licked at its rump.

"Where to now?" Jules said.

"Over here first."

Dig hitched his bag over his shoulder and threaded through the crowd to a familiar shopfront with *Helpful Hari's Tourist Information* written in the front window. He pushed through the curtain of beads in the doorway. Hari was sitting in his usual position behind the desk, scratching at his sideburns, his tie hanging loosely around his neck. His nephew sat at one of the computers with headphones on. *Call of Duty* gunfire burst across the screen. As Dig walked in Hari frowned.

"You," he said. "You owe me one bicycle."

"Yes, I do. But the bad news is I can't bring it back to you. It was lost."

Hari lifted a finger in the air. "You'll have to pay. Two thousand rupee."

"Fair enough." Dig extracted his wallet and handed over the money.

Hari took the cash, inspected it, and waggled his head with a smile. "Very good," he said. "Now is there anything else I can do for you? Train ticket? Bus ticket?"

"First, I'd like to make a phone call home."

"Of course."

"Then I'd like to hire a motorbike."

Hari's smile dropped.

They were on the road soon after, with Dig in control of the motorbike and Jules hooked in behind him, her arms tight around his waist. The bike threw up gravel as they weaved through the centre of the bazaar.

Jules leaned into Dig's ear and spoke loudly over the roar of the engine. Her hair blew behind her in the slipstream. "How far away is it?"

"About half an hour," Dig shouted, "But it'll be a pretty bumpy ride."

Jules' grip tightened around his waist. "Have we got this right?"

Dig shrugged, and turned his attention to the road.

They followed the trail to the old railway line, then Dig slowed the bike and turned left to rumble down the centre of the tracks. The air was dry and dusty, and thick bushes lined the tracks on both sides.

As they travelled, a familiar fluttering grew in his stomach. He realised that everything was now on the line—not just his own life, but the lives of Jules, Chook, and his family. His whole world was hedged on his hunch regarding Raj.

But was his hunch correct? And could he even prove it? And if it was true, what value did the secret hold to Maxine?

He didn't know. But he knew he had to try. Otherwise they would be back, in Dig's own home, and dishing out retribution on Maxine's own terms. Dig gritted his teeth and focused on the centre of the railway tracks. It was time to face it all head on.

The track dipped down across the low wooden river bridge, and the motorbike wheel bounced through the sleepers. As he steered the bike up the opposite bank, Dig glanced toward the cluster of broken bushes where he had crashed Shiv's motorbike on the way out.

The track straightened and directed itself toward the bowels of the high, imposing hill that stood as the last line of defence between the brewery and the outside world. The rocky ridges rose up on both sides of the track and the dark crescent of the tunnel appeared ahead like a rotten sinkhole.

Dig slowed the bike to a stop outside the tunnel mouth. A warm breeze howled into their faces, like the fetid breath of the mountain itself.

"What's happening?" Jules said.

Dig took a deep breath. "The brewery's on the other side of this tunnel." He rummaged through his bag and unfolded his map. After studying it for a moment he pointed to a square on the plan ringed by closely spaced contours. "We're surrounded by cliffs here. The tunnel's the only way through."

"And they're holding Chook on the other side?"

"That's what Shiv said." He turned to her. "You ready?"

Jules blinked rapidly. Her face was white. "Just a sec." She stepped off the bike with hunched shoulders and brought her pack to her chest. She fumbled the zip open and lifted out a packet of cigarettes, then with trembling hands she extracted a thickly rolled cylinder and a lighter from the box. She placed the cigarette into her mouth and tried to fire it to life, but the wind extinguished the flame.

She turned her back to Dig, shielded herself from the wind, and attempted to light it again. Soon the familiar, sweet musky smell filled the air.

Dig opened his mouth to speak, then closed it, and just shook his head minutely.

Jules turned. "I don't know Dig, I've got a bad feeling about this." She took another drag on her cigarette. "It just feels like we're walking into a big trap."

"You don't have to come. You can wait here if you like."

Jules grimaced. "I've got to get Chook..." She swallowed. "Look, how about this. We go in, and I just hand back all the cash and gear I stole and we ask for a truce."

"I thought you said there was no more?"

Jules' eyes narrowed. She stood with one arm across her midriff and an elbow propped up holding the burning cigarette. She turned her back to him again; the protruding tag on the back of her shirt was still visible against her neckline.

"How'd you get the stuff past that checkpoint?"

Jules remained silent.

Dig ran a hand through his hair, then his attention returned to Jules' shirt tag. He kicked out the bike stand and stepped off the machine.

"Did you say that you got that shirt made up in Badami?"

Jules glanced at him, then tried to push the lighter back into the cigarette packet with a shaking hand. "Yeah that's right."

"So why do you have a *Made in China* tag on the back of it?"

The lighter fell clattering to the timbers between the tracks. The tendons in Jules' neck tightened and she reached to the back of her neck to tuck the tag away.

Dig frowned. "So what did you..." He took a quick intake of breath. "Your bag...you had him do something to your bag. To hide the opium you stole."

Jules scowled. "You should keep your head out of my business." She glanced at the pack on Dig's shoulders as she walked back toward the bike. "Let's just go find my brother."

Dig followed her gaze to his pack. A heavy feeling settled in his stomach. "No," he said. "You didn't. Did you?"

He whipped off his bag and dumped it on the ground between his legs, then ripped open the zip and pushed the contents about inside, pressing his hand against the inside walls. Jules' eyes widened.

Dig continued to search—and then he found it, a patch of rough, thick stitching around a piece of fabric that did not match the rest of the material. He pulled at it, and the material tore away, revealing a flat, hard block wrapped in plastic wrap.

He glared at her. "When I went for my walk in Badami," he seethed. "*You sewed drugs into my bag?* And left me to carry them through the checkpoint for you?" Heat flushed through his body and he stepped toward Jules with his fists clenched. She cowered away and took a couple of unbalanced steps down the track ballast.

"How dare you!" Dig shouted, breathing rapidly with his feet wide apart. Blood pounded in his ears.

Jules clambered across the toe of the ballast, heading toward the tunnel, then climbed it again and stood beside the bike. "Listen," she said, holding her palms out in front of her. "It's our back up plan...if things go bad we can try to trade it for our lives. Get things back to how they were. I can make it up with Shiv if I want, I know it."

"And what happens to me in that scenario? You offer me up as a sacrifice?"

"No." Jules' eyebrows drew together. "You can...join the business too."

"Are you crazy? Are you ever going to face reality? Your time is *over* out here. You need to ditch the drugs, find Chook, and go home."

Jules blinked rapidly and looked down to her feet—where Dig's bag lay on the ground beside the bike. Her lips pursed.

Dig stepped toward her. "Don't you da—"

But it was too late. Jules snatched up Dig's pack, then turned to mount the motorbike. She started it up and threw the bike into gear.

Dig ran at her, pumping his arms and legs and sprinting down the centre of the track. When he was within arm's reach he grabbed for the back of the bike, but she pulled back the throttle and it shot away toward the tunnel, wavering back and forth between the rails.

"Stop!" Dig shouted. "Just wait!" He chased her down the line. "There are hornets in there! *Hornets!*" But the bike zipped away into the gaping hole of the tunnel, and Dig jogged to a stop outside the opening.

He watched the rear lights of the motorbike disappear into the depths of the hill until he was left only with the dissipating buzz of the engine as it echoed back toward him. Dig laced his hands on the top of his head and stared into the darkness.

As he stood, the echo suddenly changed pitch, then hitched and caught, and for an awful second there was a zinging pause before an almighty crash of broken plastic and metal echoed down the passage.

Then a puttering hiss.

Then silence.

Dig took two running steps into the tunnel opening before spotting a couple of roaming insects zipping through the shadows.

He looked down at his bare arms and legs and stopped, frozen. All his spare clothes had been taken with the stolen pack. All his medicines had gone with it too. He could go no further.

A familiar sound began to ramp up ahead of him—like the vibrant hum of an electrical substation, cranking up through the gears, emitting an unnerving pulsation that reverberated in his chest. Dig knew what it was; it was the sound of the hive coming to life, ready to attack. Ready to inflict pain.

A primal, high-pitched scream echoed back from the tunnel, making the hairs on the back of Dig's neck stand to attention.

"Get them off me!" Jules' voice echoed, whimpering.

Dig's breathing increased, and he paced back and forth at the tunnel mouth. "Run Jules!" he shouted into the tunnel. "Run!"

"They're everywhere," she squealed. "Help me!"

"I can't! You need to get out!"

There was a guttural moan, and a slapping, followed by a series of sobs.

"Stop them!" she screamed. "Just…stop…!"

He continued to pace. "Get out of there!" he screamed into the darkness.

"I…can't! Oh…please!…Help meee!"

"Run to my voice!"

But there was no answer. All he could hear was the humming ferocity of the hive, churning at full intensity somewhere around the corner in the darkness. His legs felt weak, and he dropped to a squatting position just outside the tunnel opening, eyes screwed shut and full of moisture. He shook his head.

A final word screamed out of the tunnel mouth in an ear splitting shriek, echoing off the tunnel walls and drilling into his brain.

"Pleeeeeeeeeeeeeeeeeee…"

Dig crammed his thumbs into his ear canals and squashed his palms hard against his temples until his head throbbed. His eyes screwed shut and nausea churned in his stomach.

"…eeeeeeeeeeeeeeeeeee…"

He willed the sound to stop, but it continued on and on, for a near implausible length of time, piercing through his head and jamming his thoughts until finally it trailed away, and he was left with nothing but the humming echo of the hive.

He dropped backwards to lie on his back, with the twin metal strips of the train line running past each shoulder. The timber sleepers were warm below his shoulder blades, and he stared blankly at the clouds floating past the arch of the tunnel opening. Tears tracked over his cheekbones and pooled at his earlobes.

He felt spent, like all his willpower had been depleted.

His mind was blank, and he didn't have the energy to start it again.

As he stared at the sky, his vision caught on a small, colourful shape moving through the air, turning circles in the breeze. It ducked and dived, then glided toward him and landed cleanly on the top of the tunnel arch above his head. It was a bird, and Dig felt no surprise when he recognised it as a Rainbow Bee Eater. It lifted its wing and preened its undercarriage, then looked sideways at him.

Dig watched the bird with a trembling chin, then closed his eyes and pressed his lips thinly together.

"Why?" he whispered, as another tear tracked down his cheek. "Why did you have to go and die Dad? And leave us this shitfight to deal with?"

He sniffed. "Well I give up. I'm going home. The brewery can go to shit. And if they come after us, then so be it." He took a deep breath. "I can't get through that tunnel. I'll be eaten alive." He looked up at the bird. It remained on the top of the arch, unmoved.

"So that's it," he said. "No more."

The bird cocked its head, then launched into the air and flew toward Hampi. Dig sat up and watched it leave, his eyebrows knitting together.

He waited, listening to the howl of the wind in the tunnel. But the bird didn't return.

"Fine." Dig pushed himself to his feet. He wiped at his cheeks and walked down the tracks, away from the tunnel, away from the brewery.

He followed the tracks around the bend, stepping slowly from one sleeper to the next. His head throbbed. Out of habit, he reached for his water bottle, but of course it was gone too, sitting inside his pack that was now likely somewhere in the depths of hornet hill. He shuffled along the sleepers with his head down, sweat dripping from his eyebrows, his mouth dry and tasting of dirt. He considered how far he had left to walk, and he realised he would probably be close to dehydration by the time he got back to town.

And what else was in the pack? His passport for one, his money and credit card. How would he get out of the country? He frowned and stopped.

The track dipped down to the right, heading for the bridge over the river. Flanking the bend was the pocket of broken palms where he had lost control of the motorbike days before. The motorbike would still be in there somewhere, mangled and lifeless against the trunk of the palm.

He narrowed his eyes, then glanced at the towering hill of rock behind him. Its base was steep and slippery, and would be impossible to climb. The breeze from the tunnel still whined in his face.

After a moment, Dig stepped carefully down the ballast shoulder to the tree line. When he reached the palms, he found the broken branches that marked his crash entry point, and stuck his head through the gap into the shadows beyond.

After his eyes adjusted, he saw it—the mangled wreck of metal that was the motorbike, already tangled in spider webs and surrounded by a dark ring of dirt that was likely motor oil from a fractured engine. Dig ducked his head, stepped through the branches, and pushed his way through the foliage toward the bike.

He walked around to the rear of the bike and spotted what he was looking for—the open storage compartment under the bike seat—and the pair of worn overalls and scuffed helmet that had spilt out of it during the crash a couple of days earlier.

He grabbed a cuff of the overalls and pulled them toward him, but they stuck fast, hooked somewhere underneath the main body of the bike. He crouched to the forest floor, levered his shoulder below the main frame, and pushed up. The bike protested with a squeal of metal-on-metal, but lifted, and Dig yanked the overalls free. He lowered the bike to the ground and held the garment up to the light. It was dirty and worn, but seemed intact.

He picked up the helmet. The paint was chipped and the visor cracked, but it was still in one piece. He rubbed at the visor with his shirt, then tried it on for size. It pressed hard against his ears, but he managed to squeeze it on before removing it again.

He stared at the two items for another long moment, then took a deep breath and pressed his lips together before he lifted his T-shirt over his head and dropped it in a pile beside him. He stepped into the overalls, inserted his arms, and drew the front zipper up tightly to the underside of his chin, then tucked the bottom of the overalls into his socks. The garment was a couple of sizes too small and pulled down at the top of his shoulders—but it covered him from his ankles to his wrists to his chin.

From the ground, he lifted a solid branch that was the length of his arm, then collected a litter of dry palm fronds and began tying them to the stick. When he was finished, he had a thick wrapping of dried leaf tied around the top half.

He lifted the helmet and shirt from the ground and pushed his way out of the foliage to climb back up the embankment. When he reached the railway line he put his head down and trudged toward the hill, stick in one hand, helmet and shirt in the other.

The track turned a now familiar bend back into the hill, and the rocky outcroppings again rose up on both sides of the track. Dig gritted his teeth as the semicircle of darkness appeared around the bend.

As he neared the tunnel entrance the breeze increased in intensity, blowing a hot, rotten blast that flapped his hair across his face and smelled of stagnant water and decomposition.

He stopped and stared into the dark. A wave of goose bumps broke out across his arms and his stomach churned. He placed the stick carefully on the ground with a shaking hand, and lifted his T- shirt up to wrap it tightly around the base of his neck. He held the helmet out, swallowed, then squashed it down onto his head. The interior stank of sweat and motor oil.

Scratches in the visor blurred his vision, and the thick crack ran diagonally across his line of sight—but he could see enough to keep himself orientated. He traced his fingers along the joints of the helmet, searching for exposed sections of skin around his neck, until he convinced himself that he was as ready as he could be.

He crouched and searched amongst the rails. Eventually he found what he was looking for—a small green lighter wedged beside a battered railway sleeper, the same lighter that Jules had dropped minutes earlier. He stood at the tunnel entrance, breathing shallowly and already sweating profusely inside the clothing—then flicked the lighter to life and brought it to the top of the stick.

The closest of the dried palm fronds flickered into flame, and it spread quickly across the top of the stick, creating a burning, crackling fire that billowed smoke in a plume above his head.

The rank breeze upped another notch and blew into his face, howling from somewhere deep within the hill. Embers flew from his makeshift torch and lodged into his clothing. Dig flicked them away, then tucked both hands into the arms of his overalls and walked into the darkness.

As the walls closed in around him the torch glowed orange with a new intensity, fuelled by the headwind, throwing flames and smoke back towards him. He held the torch out in front, trying to direct the glowing cinders away from his head.

Shadows danced across the walls and his eyes darted left and right, trying to make sense of the shapes through the tint of the scratched visor. But he kept walking forward, down the centre of the tracks, into the heart of the mountain.

As he turned the first bend, the unsettling hum increased, and a shiver tracked down between his shoulder blades. The first hornets appeared in the air, orbiting frantic circles around the torch. One landed in the centre of his visor, and he flinched. From this angle he could see its gruesome body up close—a writhing hairy mass of gold and black stripes with stinger prodding into the lens.

Dig breathed shallowly and his heart raced. His breath spread semicircles of moisture across his visor, blocking his vision. He waved his makeshift torch at his face and the hornet disappeared into the smoke, only to be replaced by three more crawling across the lens.

More insects crawled near his ears, their tiny feet dancing across the helmet and buzzing so loudly it seemed they were burrowing into his canal.

But he kept walking, step by step, holding the torch ahead of him, trying to maintain sight of the tracks, leaning into the whining, stinking headwind that seemed to grow stronger with each step.

The tunnel straightened, and through the storm of insects he spotted a circle of light on the base of his vision. He recognised the old timber signal box hanging on the ceiling, housing the swarming blackness of the nest.

His heart raced and blood pounded in his ears; stars danced across his vision. He realised he was breathing too fast, and he forced himself to slow his intake until his vision returned to some type of normality.

The buzzing whine of the hive increased to a fevered intensity. A dark cyclone of insects swirled in the air above it. Then, as he moved within spitting distance, they came at him.

In an instant he was enveloped—his vision blanked out by a threefold layer of hornets squirming across the visor. He felt them digging at the fabric around his neck, squeezing into the gaps between his toes, and covering his body in a writhing heavy weight that felt like a thick, warm layer of screaming fury.

Dig moaned through gritted teeth, but the noise was drowned away by the insects swarming around his ears—a sound that had moved beyond a buzz or a whine; it was the sound of a screaming engine redlining into overdrive.

Dig lifted the torch to his face and his vision momentarily cleared. He spotted a glimpse of rail at his feet and pushed on, one step at a time, until he was again aware of the circle of light ahead of him, down to his right, on the side of tracks. He waved his torch toward it, and through the cloud of insects he saw a glint of bent steel tubing and rubber tyre. It was the motorbike, lying upside down with the wheel rims buckled.

He pushed past the bike to stand at the base of the weathered timber cabinet. Nestled in the top of the cabinet was the cylindrical mass of the overflowing, fibrous hive. A dark hole punctuated its base, and a ferocious sea of hornets poured out.

Dig lowered his torch and stepped forward again, and the light passed a patch of pale skin on the ground. He returned his torch to it, and took a sharp intake of breath.

Jules' pink face stared up, blotched and swollen, with vacant eyes and a thick purple tongue. Parallel tracks of rutted, dried blood ran from cheekbone to chin, with a limp hand lying beside; the fingernails were matted in red and choked with clumps of skin.

She lay on her back with her legs sprawled. Her shirt was hitched up, exposing a swollen midriff covered in raised purple welts and small black puncture marks of dried blood. One foot was twisted sideways at the ankle—likely broken. Bile rose in Dig's throat, and he gagged.

When he regained his composure, he glanced back at her. Through the clouded lens of his helmet he saw some form of shadow moving on her face, but he couldn't pinpoint its nature.

He wanted to run, but instead he moved the torch in closer to get a better look—and through the mass of flying insects he realised it was more than a shadow—there was a lump moving behind her cheek.

The lump tracked slowly to the corner of her mouth, then Jules' upper lip curled away to reveal two murky brown eyes set against an oversized bright orange head. Sharp mandibles hung from the maw of the creature, and they opened and closed like a pair of jagged scissors.

An icy chill ran down his spine as the insect studied him, and Dig sensed what it was. It was a hornet, but this one was bigger and meaner than the rest of the swarm. It was the queen.

He again felt the urge to run—to leave the tunnel and never come back. But he couldn't. His grip tightened on the torch until his knuckles ached, and he bunched his shoulders over Jules' body. A hot flush of rage rose through the back of his neck, blinding him of any logical thought.

Memories flashed across his mind. Memories of sitting at the waterhole while his father choked the wasp from his mouth to the rock platform, changing his life forever. Memories of pain and fear as he was stung on the elbow while he sat on the roof of the house. Memories of terror as he steered the motorbike through the wall of writhing hornets a few days before.

He leaned forward and waved the torch toward the queen. "Get out of there!" he shouted, his voice muffled inside the helmet. Insects churned around him, flying kamikaze into his head, bouncing off his visor.

The queen watched him, her mandibles opening and shutting, then slowly extracted herself from Jules' mouth. The long black wings emerged first, and a bulbous orange and black striped abdomen followed. She climbed to the bridge of Jules' nose, stood on her hind legs, and extended her wings wide, seemingly taunting him.

Dig pulled the torch back, then thrust it forward like a fencing sword; it struck the queen and knocked her from her perch. The insect dropped away in a blur of wings and turned an upward arc toward his head, then ricocheted solidly off the centre of the plastic visor.

Dig cried out and waved his torch in front of his face. The queen vanished amongst the swarm before thumping into his visor a second time. Dig gritted his teeth and swiped at the air again—and felt the impact of a glancing blow. She landed heavily on the base of the hive, stretched one shaky wing, then crawled back into the depths of the nest.

The timber cabinet framing the nest was splintered and pocked with termite holes. Dig panted, arms heavy from the layers of insects writhing across them, and pushed the torch up to the base of the frame. The flames flickered and then caught, and rose up the rectangular box toward the hive.

A flurry of hornets flew around him in a thick wave of panic, their wings beating manically like an aircraft jet firing up for takeoff. Insects lifted from his body and flew directly into the flames, catching alight and dropping to the floor in writhing balls of fire.

Dig took a few ragged breaths, then waved the torch down to his feet and found the tracks again, re-orientating himself. He started to walk.

He took a few steps before he remembered Jules' body, lying alone beside the burning cabinet. He winced, then stepped back to crouch beside her. Heat from the fire radiated through his clothes. From the hive, a high pitched whine increased in intensity, like a kettle coming to the boil.

Dig placed his torch on the ground, then grabbed Jules beneath her armpits, hoisting her to a sitting position. A black lump of fabric lay behind her—his pack. He blinked rapidly as an idea formed in his mind, then he pulled the bag open and fished out his water bottle. He tipped out the contents and swiped the open bottle through the cloud of insects, closed it tightly, and replaced it in the bag.

After swinging the pack over his back he hoisted Jules' body over one shoulder, pushed up to his feet, and stepped away from the burning hive.

Dig struggled to balance her weight. His chest wheezed and sweat tracked down his ribs beneath the layers of clothing.

Behind him, the hive emitted an ear piercing wail, and something crackled and popped, then fell to the tunnel floor with a crash. Dig trudged onward with the muscles in his back cramping and the inside of the helmet visor near clouded over with moisture. Finally, the semi-circle of the tunnel exit appeared ahead of him. He lumbered towards it.

When he reached the opening, the sunlight bit at his eyes and he threw the torch to the floor. He stopped and lowered Jules' body to the ground, just inside the shade of the opening, seating her against the tunnel wall.

He ripped the helmet from his head. His hair was matted in sweat and his face flushed. He dropped his hands to his knees, panting, trying to recover his breath.

After a while, he straightened and stared into the depths of the tunnel. The wind was gone, the air still. Smoke drifted out of the crown of the tunnel and floated into the sky.

Dig wiped at his face with the back of his arm, then unzipped the overalls and peeled them off his body. He turned to Jules, still propped up against the wall of the tunnel, her head tilted sideways and staring at the sky—and his brow furrowed.

He walked over to stand beside her. After a moment, he cleared his throat.

"I'm going to leave you here for a bit," he said. "But...someone will back for you later on." The echo of water trickled down a wall within the tunnel. "I'm sorry," he said. "For everything. It wasn't supposed to end like this. But I'll go and find Chook now. I promise you that."

He scratched at the back of his neck, then turned, picked up his pack, and stepped out of the tunnel opening into the sunlight. The breeze cooled the sweat across his temples.

Ahead of him, the rail line followed the ridge as it eased down toward the river. A flock of white birds tracked across a hazy sky, and thunder rumbled behind the clouds. On the river's edge, nestled amongst the trees, stood the boxy shape of the brewery and the small rectangular house. To his left, the rail embankment dropped steeply down to the wide expanse of hop fields across the meadow.

He retrieved his water bottle from his bag. It vibrated in his grasp—the trapped hornets fighting to get out, before he pushed it carefully into the pocket of his shorts. He then fished the two Epipens out of his pack—the same ones his mother had given him as he left Australia—and slotted them into the opposite pocket.

He dropped to his rear and slid down through the loose rocks of the ballast shoulder until he came to a stop at the first rows of leafy green hops.

The vines climbed high above his head, supported by stretches of regularly spaced cable that spanned out across the field. Heart shaped leaves with finely toothed edges spread evenly up the vines. Deep green hops sprouted from the base of the leaves, filling the air with a sweet, musky, bitter fragrance.

He stepped into the field of plants, and with leaves tugging at his shoulders he walked deep into the centre of the crop—heading for the house.

18

THE GROUND BELOW THE VINES was loose and loamy, and sunk under his feet as he moved between the plants. The vines blocked out the sky, but he kept his bearings by walking parallel to the rectangular grid of crops. The bitter aroma of the hops enveloped him, triggering memories of the refrigerated storage area back home. He stopped often to regain his breath and maintain his composure. Was it possible the smell of the hops alone was making him lightheaded?

Eventually, the cables supporting the vines dropped to the ground in a long straight row at the edge of the meadow. Dig approached the boundary carefully, hopping amongst the shadows from vine to vine until he could make out the rectangular shape of the house, not far past the edge of the crop. The building was nestled amongst the line of banyan trees that grew on the bank of the river. From behind the house, he could hear the trickle of flowing water.

A group of motorbikes were lined up at the house, and three men sat at a table near the front door—talking, drinking and playing cards. Dig recognised the silhouette of Shiv sitting against the house, facing him. The bulky frames of the thugs sat before him.

Dig crept back into the depths of the crop, then flanked the edge of the house, out of sight of the men.

From there he skipped across the dirt and jumped into the cool shadows of the banyan trees by the river. Hidden frogs croaked in a steady rhythm beneath his feet.

He checked for activity at the house before creeping along the water's edge behind the trees, his feet leaving liquid filled footprints in the wet sand.

The curtains on the rear glass doors were pulled back, exposing the pale cement walls and timber ceiling beams of the living room and kitchen.

Raj sat at the stone kitchen counter with his back to Dig, writing on a pad of paper, talking. His father, Girish, stood on the opposite side of the bench. Glass tumblers were lined up on the table. Girish's nose wrinkled as he crouched and poured measured amounts into the cups from an unlabelled bottle in his hand.

A rasping female voice echoed through the house, and Raj and Girish turned to the hallway as Maxine sauntered into view. Dig's stomach clenched as he spotted her.

She stood with a tight jaw and her arms folded. Her lank hair was pulled back behind her head, but tracts had broken free and hung loosely down the side of a greasy face.

Girish scampered over to her, placed a hand behind the small of her back, and led her to the kitchen bench. She scowled and tried to turn back, but Girish gestured again toward the glasses on the table.

Maxine rolled her eyes and dropped into a chair, then lifted a glass to her lips.

Girish and Raj watched with bright eyes as she emptied the glass and returned it to the counter. She nodded, and stood.

Girish returned his hand to her back and tried to coax her back into the seat, but she flapped a hand in dismissal and barked at him. Girish cowered, and she headed back into the hall and out of sight.

Girish watched her leave, then glanced at Raj. Raj gave a half-hearted shrug.

Dig watched the exchange and felt a pang of regret. If he was right with his assumptions, the boy was his half-brother. Was he prepared to destroy the relationship between Girish and Raj for the sake of his own family unit back home? If he needed to, then yes, he certainly would. But if he could get Maxine alone, then maybe it could be avoided.

He needed to talk to her. Could he sneak into the house, track her down before he was detected, and convince her to speak to him without raising an alarm? It seemed a near impossible task.

Girish picked up the empty glass from the counter and moved it to the sink. Raj returned to writing in his notepad. Dig made his move.

He pushed through the overhanging roots of the banyan tree and hoisted himself onto the back deck. Glass clattered against the sink as he dropped his shoes to the ground.

Dig peeked around the door jamb, then dropped to his hands and knees and crawled through the doorway.

The bare concrete floor was cool, and the twang of a sitar echoed from speakers on the ceiling. To his left, a set of couches and a heavy timber coffee table flanked the corner of the room. As he glanced to the right, he took a sharp intake of breath.

A doorway led into the small bathroom of rendered cement where he had showered on his previous visit to the house. Chook sat slumped in the corner of the room, his head tilted to his shoulder. His face was smeared with dirt and blood. One arm was tied to a solid metal towel rack above his head. Red stains covered his torn shirt. After thinking for a moment, Dig crawled into the room.

Chook looked up, startled. He tried to straighten and winced, then slumped back down. His tied arm was fixed awkwardly above his head, and the other lay across his chest, protecting the red and swollen stub on his hand. An odour of rotting meat hung in the air.

Dig put a finger to his lips, then examined Chook's restricted arm. It was fixed tight to the metal bar by a thick cable tie. The plastic had sliced a red ring into his skin and tinged his hand a shade of purple.

He turned his attention to the towel rack. It was held in place by four screws, and Dig picked at them with his fingernail. He blinked before fishing a handful of change out of his pocket. One of the silver coins was thin, and marked as one Indian rupee.

He glanced through the doorway, then held the coin up to the first screw and twisted. Initially the screw hung tight, but then it gave up its resistance and twisted out of the wall. Dig copied this action with the remaining screws, and the solid towel rack fell into Dig's hand. He lowered the bar to the floor and unhooked the cable tie from Chook's wrist. Chook grimaced and rubbed his trembling arm against his shirt.

Wait here okay? Dig mouthed. Chook nodded weakly and closed his eyes.

Dig crept back to the doorway and peered around the opening. Raj remained seated with his back to him, and Girish was rummaging through the fridge. The hallway opening stood about ten steps away.

He dropped to his haunches and tiptoed across the concrete. Raj leaned back in his seat and the frame squealed against the vinyl.

Dig kept moving, treading slowly past Raj's back, almost within arm's reach, and ducked into the dim light of the hallway. He stood with his back against one wall, taking deep breaths.

Pictures hung on the hallway walls at regular intervals. A photo of a woman in her early twenties faced him. In it, she wore jeans and her long dark hair fell loose over her healthy frame. She leaned against a railing with the backdrop of the Hampi hills behind her. Her eyes were strong and mischievous, and Dig recognised her as a young, seemingly innocent version of Maxine. He stared at the picture, wondering how she had become the bitter relic of a woman that she was today.

Maybe I'll find out, he considered, because now it was time. Time to face Maxine and put all the drama to rest, one way or another. He squared himself up, and turned down the hall.

He took two steps before he froze. Ahead of him on the floor, sitting in a worn wicker basket, was Maxine's dog, Digit.

The dog sat up straight and studied Dig with pointed ears. A cream plaster cast encased his front leg; one shoulder was shaved and covered in a brown paste.

Dig's heart pounded. He held his palms out in front of him. "Hey!" he whispered. "Hey boy!"

A rumble grew from the dog's throat; its lips curled up to reveal stained and pointed canines.

"It's okay," Dig whispered. "Relax!"

The dog growled and gave a bark, echoing down the hall.

The movement from the main room ceased and a quiet hung in the air, save for the low tune of the sitar playing on the stereo.

"Digit?" Chair legs scraped against the concrete.

Dig stood poised, his eyes darting back and forth between the dog and the main room.

The dog barked again, loudly.

Dig winced as Raj appeared in the hallway. His mouth dropped open.

"Hi Raj," Dig said in a strained voice. "Now just let me explain okay?"

Raj's eyes bulged. "Shiv!" he exclaimed in a stuttering shout. "Everyone! It's him!" Dig pursed his lips and took a step backward.

Girish appeared in the hallway behind Raj, eyebrows furrowed. He blinked rapidly, then joined in the chorus. "Shiv!" he shouted. "Get in here!"

A door squealed open and a rumble of footsteps echoed through the house. "What?"

"In here!"

Shiv appeared in the doorway with his shoulders wide, panting. "What the...?" He clenched his hands into fists as his two companions appeared behind him.

"Now wait a sec," Dig said, holding his palms up. "I'm not here to hurt anyone. Just talk."

The bald-headed thug burst forward and yanked Dig's arm behind his back. Shiv backhanded Dig across the face, clouding his vision and knocking him to the floor.

He was hauled across the concrete by one arm; the floor felt like sandpaper on his knees. He tasted blood in his mouth. Someone lifted him by the armpits and dumped him onto the stool by the kitchen counter.

Before he could reach for the water bottle in his pocket, a cable tie zipped tight around his wrist, fixing him to the frame of the seat. This action was copied on his other extremities until he was tied to the seat by both wrists and ankles. Blood pumped in his temples, and he tipped his head back to take a few breaths while he waited for the ringing in his ears to subside.

Clicking heels echoed from the hallway, and everyone in the room straightened. Maxine emerged through the doorway with the dog under one arm. Her eyes were underscored by dark rings, but still gleamed with a fevered intensity. A double chin bulged at her neckline.

She placed the dog on the ground, then produced a packet of cigarettes from a hip pocket. She lifted a cigarette to her mouth and fired it up—the end glowing bright as she drew in the smoke. She exhaled a cloud in front of her, then glanced at Shiv. "He broke into the house?"

Shiv nodded.

Maxine grabbed Shiv's earlobe between two fingers and yanked it sideways. He grimaced and his hands hovered at his head, then dropped back down. A flush ran across his cheeks.

Maxine breathed smoke into his face. "Not good enough," she said, and released him.

Maxine walked across to Dig and stood over him, smirking. Dig glanced up through a lowered brow.

"You again," Maxine said.

"Thanks for the invite."

She took another drag on her cigarette. "Where's your girlfriend?"

Dig felt Shiv's eyes on him, and he blinked. "She wasn't my girlfriend," he said. "But she won't be coming. She had an accident."

Shiv tilted up his chin. "What kind of accident?"

"She fell off the motorbike in the tunnel. She didn't make it back out."

"You're lying," Maxine said.

"I'm not."

She narrowed her eyes. "That's easily checked." She looked to Shiv. He was staring blankly out the window, his lips thin. She rolled her eyes and turned to the bald-headed thug—he nodded and walked out of the room.

Maxine turned back to Dig. "And you've come here to give yourself up?"

"No," Dig said, and kept her gaze. "I came here to offer you a deal."

She raised her eyebrows and scoffed.

"I think we both want the same thing," Dig continued. "To keep our family safe and...together."

She stared at him. "You think you can threaten me? While tied up like a pig?"

Dig blinked and glanced around the room. "I'm not talking about physical harm," he said. "I'm talking about keeping *secrets* safe. *Family* secrets."

Maxine stiffened and her eyes cut toward Girish. She lifted her cigarette to her lips and took a long drag. She looked out the glass doors to the river, then turned to the other people in the room. "Leave us for a moment."

Girish and Raj frowned at each other. "But—"

"Leave!" Maxine shouted with a hand on her hip. "Now."

Girish shook his head and gestured toward Raj. "Come on." They walked out to stand on the deck. Shiv and the bald-headed thug followed behind.

When the room was empty, Maxine placed her cigarette into an ashtray on the bench, then walked to the kitchen and pulled a beer from the fridge door. She popped off the top and took a mouthful.

"Listen," Dig whispered. "If you hurt me today, your family finds out the truth. My brother's ready to make a phone call if he doesn't hear from me by nightfall."

She watched him for a moment. "And what truth is that?"

He glanced toward the deck. "I'll make sure that Raj finds out we shared a father."

Maxine's eyes flared.

"But, if you leave me and Chook alone, we'll forget we ever came here, and you'll never see us again. You have my word."

She lifted the cigarette to her lips and squinted into the smoke.

"Do we have an understanding?"

Maxine nodded slowly. "Yes. I think I understand."

Dig let out a breath. "Good."

An unbalanced smile broke out across her lips. "I understand you're even more dense than I thought!" She smirked, then turned toward the balcony. "Girish! Get back in here."

Girish hesitated, then walked back into the room to stand beside them.

"Hold out your hands."

Girish frowned and folded his arms. "Would you mind telling me—"

"Just hold them out!"

Girish flinched, then slowly lifted his hands out for inspection.

Max turned to Dig and pointed. "Look."

Girish gave a pinched expression and stared at the ceiling. Dig looked at his arms. While Girish's natural skin colour was dark, the back of his hands and fingers were covered in blotchy patches of white.

"Do you know what Vitiligo is?" Maxine said.

Dig shook his head.

"Well, now you do. It's a skin condition that causes an ugly white depigmentation."

Girish pursed his lips and dropped his hands back into his pockets.

"You now," she shouted across the room to where Raj was standing. "Come here."

Raj shuffled over and stood beside Girish. They exchanged a look.

Max took another mouthful from her beer. "Now look at these two unfortunate specimens. And tell me they're not father and son."

Dig looked from Girish to Raj and back again, and butterflies churned in his stomach. The two had thin frames, bushy eyebrows and protruding Adam's Apples. They also shared the same shade of skin. It was near impossible they were not related.

"Now you," she said to Raj. "Hands."

Raj scowled, and slowly lifted his hands.

Dig knew what he was going to see, but he looked anyway. Raj's hands were dark and calloused, but the fingers and back of his palms were covered in the same patches of blotchy white.

Raj retracted his hands, folded them across his chest, and stared at Dig like he was a stranger. Which, it seemed, he was.

Maxine turned to Dig. "Vitiligo is hereditary. As, it seems, is stupidity—between you and your father."

Dig's pulse raced. "You did know him then."

"Of course I knew him," she said, curtly. "In a business capacity. He came into the bar many years ago, *demanding* we let him import our hops. He was a simple man. But thick-headed."

"So why did you agree?"

Maxine picked up her beer and turned to walk slowly toward the balcony. "Everything has a price," she said. "And he was prepared to pay for it. If he took care of the extraction for us, and passed on the product in Australia—then he could use our hops."

Dig frowned. "But...that just doesn't seem like him."

Maxine strode back to Dig and leaned over him. "Get it into your head you idiot! Your father was no saint. He was greedy. And he gambled his life away for his business."

Dig clenched his teeth and moisture welled in the corner of his eyes. He shook his head minutely.

"And you've done the same. Gambled the lives of your family away for money." She smirked. "And lost."

Dig looked up, eyes wide. "Look," he said. "This whole thing was just me okay? My family have nothing to do with it—so you can leave them out of it."

Maxine took another mouthful from the bottle. "Sorry boy," she said. "We can't take that chance."

The rumble of an engine approached outside, followed by the squeaking brakes of the hi-rail truck as it pulled to a stop. A door opened and then slammed shut. The bald-headed thug walked in, supporting a wrapped tarpaulin across the front of his chest. He raised his eyebrows at Maxine, and then placed the tarpaulin carefully on the floor in the centre of the room.

Shiv entered from the balcony and stared down at the lumpy length of material with his eyebrows knitted together.

"You found something?" Maxine said.

The thug nodded. He reached down and pulled the top of the tarpaulin away, revealing Jules' pocked and swollen face. Her cheeks were blue and her lips cracked. Her lifeless eyes stared up at the ceiling.

Shiv's face contorted and he brought his hand up to his mouth. He coughed and retched, then tipped forward and vomited a glut of liquid onto the floor. A slick of saliva hung from his chin as he pulled in a few ragged breaths.

Maxine shuddered and turned to Shiv. "The thief got exactly what she deserved. Don't you agree?"

Shiv straightened and wiped at his mouth. He turned away from her and walked a few steps toward the deck, arms folded, looking out the window.

Maxine watched his back with a scowl. "Are you listening to me?"

Shiv stood unmoved.

Maxine strode into his field of vision. "You know whose fault this is?"

Shiv's lips thinned.

"His," Maxine said, and pointed to Dig, still tied to the chair. "He came over here, meddled in our business, and turned her against us. He is to blame."

Shiv met Maxine's gaze, then turned and narrowed his eyes at Dig.

Maxine leaned into his ear. "It's time to punish him."

Shiv nodded slowly.

"Get the knife. And remove his windpipe."

Shiv swallowed, then shuffled across to the kitchen where he plucked a large steel kitchen knife from the bench top, then returned to stand beside Dig.

Dig's muscles tensed and his breath caught in his throat. He pulled at the ties on his arms and legs. "No," he stammered. "Please! Let me go home and you'll never see me again...I'll shut down the brewery. We can pay whatever you need. Please." Sweat tracked down the back of his neck.

Maxine dropped to sit on the couch, one arm bent up at the elbow, holding a new cigarette. "I'm going to enjoy this." Dig dropped his gaze to the floor.

Shiv weighed the knife up in his grip, and stepped toward Dig with a familiar resolve in his eyes. Again, Dig yanked at the ties binding his arms, but they held firm—there was no chance to break free. His lips trembled and his heart pounded in his ears. Was this really the place where he was going to die? How much would it hurt? Would his family even know it had happened?

Shiv stopped beside him with the knife in his hand. The curls of his hair framed his round face. He turned the blade around so it faced the floor, and lifted it for the strike.

Dig dropped his head and his vision caught on Shiv's legs. For a man from the subcontinent, they were relatively pale. He wore no shoes, and his feet were dirty. Dig's gaze focused on Shiv's toes.

The second and third digits were webbed together with skin.

His eyes widened.

Shiv held the knife primed, ready to plunge it forward into Dig's throat.

"You!" Dig exclaimed. "You're my brother!"

Shiv faltered.

"Your toe! It's webbed! Like mine." Dig waggled his foot on the ground below him.

"Finish him!" Maxine called from the couch. Her voice had raised an octave, and she was sitting upright.

"And she's your *mother?*" Dig blinked rapidly. "Yes...it all makes sense."

Shiv's arm dropped and he looked across to Maxine.

She shot up from her seat. "This is bullshit. Finish him off, or I'll do it for you."

Shiv frowned.

Dig waggled his foot again. "Look at my foot! We're related!"

Shiv's eyes dropped to study Dig's foot, then his own.

Maxine stormed across the room. She grabbed a handful of Dig's hair and yanked his head backwards. "This idiot," she seethed through clenched teeth. "Is trying to screw with your mind. Don't listen to him. Ten minutes ago he was claiming *Raj* was his brother. Now he's trying the same shit on you. He's playing you, and you're too stupid to see it."

Shiv breathed heavily. "But his toe..."

"Who cares about his toe!" she screamed. "I have a birthmark on my arm—does that mean I'm related to everyone who has the same?" Her eyes were pinpricks.

Shiv dropped his gaze to the floor.

"Now, are you going to finish this bastard off or are you going to make me do it for you?"

Shiv shook his head minutely. "I can't...think," he said, and the arm holding the knife fell to his side.

Maxine sighed and held out her hand. "Give me the knife."

Shiv dropped down to sit on the coffee table.

"Give...me...the knife!" Maxine reached out.

Dig's stomach churned. "Shiv," he said. "Now is the time. She's pushed you around your whole life."

Shiv's head lifted and he met Dig's gaze.

"Take her out," Dig said.

Shiv's forehead creased; his lips quivered and his eyes welled up with moisture. He stood up, and the knife clattered to the floor. He paced over to Dig and leaned in close, nose to nose.

"She...is...my...*mother!*" Shiv screamed. "You ask me to kill my mother?" He straightened and clenched his fist. He wound his arm back, and brought it down with all his strength. The blow slammed into Dig's chin with a painful crunch.

"She is all I have!" Tears ran down Shiv's face. He lifted his arm and punched again. It thumped into the bridge of Dig's nose, and his vision exploded.

Dig came to with his chin on his chest. Blood dripped from his nose and splashed down the front of his shirt. Shiv sat slumped on the couch, staring at his hands.

Maxine patted Shiv on the back. "It's okay. You just relax for a bit." She turned. "Raj! Get Shiv a drink." Raj nodded and walked to the fridge. "One of the new ones," she added.

Raj retrieved a fresh bottle of beer from the door, and twisted off the lid as he handed it to Shiv. "Freshly brewed."

"Aren't you going to tell him your news?"

Raj scratched at his neck. "This time," he said. "We've managed to engineer the hops with coca leaf."

Shiv looked at him blankly.

Raj raised his eyebrows. "It's got cocaine in it."

Shiv gave a nod, then lifted the bottle to his lips and took a mouthful. He swallowed and licked his lips. "Good," he said, and placed the beer on the coffee table.

Maxine retrieved the knife from the floor. "You ready now?"

Shiv nodded.

Dig clenched his teeth and looked past them, out the glass doors to the river. The green water flowed smoothly past the deck. Behind it, a breeze wafted through the tops of the trees. He thought of his family, and suddenly missed them immensely.

Above the river, he noticed the small shape of a bird fluttering in the wind, ducking and diving. It turned sharply and headed toward the house, then cruised across the deck and landed by the doorway. Its wings were blue and green, and its chest was purple. The Rainbow Bee Eater sat in the doorway and cocked its head toward Dig.

Dig gave a weak smile.

I think this is it my friend, he thought. *I'm out of ideas.*

The bird hopped into the room, its talons clicking on the concrete, and gave a loud chirp.

Maxine stopped and turned.

The bird hopped further, bouncing along the floor, until it came to a stop at Dig's feet. It chirped again loudly, twice.

Maxine turned to the dog. "Digit! Get that thing out of here!" The dog ran across the room, barking.

The bird opened its wings and flapped up to land on Dig's thigh. It pushed its beak forward to snag the cable tie around Dig's wrist, and severed it.

The dog leapt up and snapped at the bird, knocking it from its perch. A handful of blue feathers fell to the ground before it took to the air, flapping and squawking, then flew a circle around the room at head height. Maxine ducked and shrieked. The men crouched and held their hands to their heads, waving it away as it approached. The bird completed a lap of the room, then disappeared out the door to the open air. The dog scampered out after it.

Shiv stared at the doorway and frowned. "What the..."

Maxine straightened her sari. "Did that bird just..."

Shiv nodded.

"Well fix it!"

Shiv stepped forward to reach for Dig's arm.

Dig steeled himself, then dropped his freed hand to his shorts pocket. The water bottle vibrated in his grip as he fumbled the cap loose with his thumb. His stomach churned as he thrust it forward.

A cloud of hornets swirled into the air, angry and buzzing. Shiv ducked and called out.

Dig tucked his head to his chest and squinted away from the insects. When they were free, he dropped the bottle and began tugging at the tie on his opposite hand, but it was no use—he remained fixed to the chair as the hornets buzzed around his head. A stinging needle of pain pierced the skin behind his ear, and he slapped the insect away with a grimace.

Shiv fell to his rear. "They're on me!" he shouted, swiping at his face.

Raj scampered into the kitchen and returned holding an aerosol can. He crouched and sprayed a cloud of mist into the air, waving the can left and right, targeting the hornets. The vapour dissipated down and the reek of insecticide filled Dig's nostrils.

Hornets dropped to the ground in whining bundles. Shiv pushed backwards across the floor and sat against the couch, breathing hard.

Dig's shoulders tensed as the sting on his neck throbbed with discomfort. His thoughts turned to the Epipens stashed in the opposite side of his shorts, and he strained his arm across his body with his back arched, trying to get his free hand into the pocket—but they were just out of his grasp.

"Tie him back up," Maxine said.

The thick-jawed thug stepped forward and grabbed Dig's arm. Dig gritted his teeth and pushed against him, grasping for the Epipens. His fingertips brushed against the plastic of the needle before his arm was wrenched away and forced back to the arm of the seat. Moments later a cable tie was fixed back around his wrist.

Dig pulled at the ties again but it was too late. His eyebrows drew together.

Maxine turned to Shiv. "You okay?"

Shiv pulled his shirt open and studied his collarbone. "I'm stung."

Maxine examined the insects twitching on the floor. "You'll be okay. It's just a bee sting."

"Hornet sting," Dig said from behind her. "And he probably won't be okay. I know that because my father, who's also *his* father, died from a sting to the throat last week."

Shiv cleared his throat and spat onto the floor. "I'm fine."

"You're probably allergic," Dig said. "Dad passed the allergy down to me. He most likely gave it to you as well. We're both stung. And we're both going to die soon if we don't get help."

Maxine's face was ashen. "He was not his father!"

"I was with Dad when he died. It was awful. Let me help you save Shiv."

"You stupid..." She scowled and stepped forward with the knife.

"I know how to help him. I promise," Dig said. A constricting headache built in his temples. "If you kill me I can't fix him."

Maxine froze, her eyes darting between Dig and Shiv.

"I'm not allergic," Shiv said. "It's just a sting." But his voice already had a constrained tone to it.

"I think you know you are. Can you feel the hot flush in your head? I can. Pretty soon your skin will itch. The swelling won't be far behind."

Shiv shook his head. "Wrong," he said in the same scratchy tone.

"Our tongue and throat will be next. They'll swell up and screw with our breathing."

"I'm breathing just fine at the m—" A ragged cough overwhelmed him and he shivered. He glanced across at Maxine, his eyes filled with fear. He rubbed his arms—a field of goosebumps covered his skin, punctuated by patches of pink. Dig felt the same goosebumps crawling across his body; a dull ache lay heavy in his chest.

"Finally our lungs will fail," Dig said, coughing. "We won't be able to breathe. We'll suffocate in about ten minutes. I know, because I was also stung last week, and nearly died too."

Shiv tilted his head back and opened his mouth. His breath laboured in a constricted wheeze.

Maxine paced back and forth across the room. "You," she said. "This is your fault." She strode to the couch and studied Shiv. He leaned back in the seat, closed his eyes, and scratched at his arms and legs.

Maxine shook her head, then barked at Raj. "Get him some water." Raj skipped across the kitchen, filled a glass from the tap, and brought it back.

Shiv took the glass and began to drink, but coughed, choking the water out onto his shirt. He closed his puffy eyes and frowned.

"Last chance," Dig croaked. He squinted into the light streaming through the exterior door. "I know how to save him, but you need to untie me."

Maxine marched abruptly across to Dig, the knife still in her hand. She leaned in close, smelling of stale sweat and mouldy breath. "You start talking, or I'll feed you your own eyeballs." She placed the tip of the knife against his cheek.

Dig sat rigidly in his chair, watching the knife from the corner of his eye. The left side of his head ached; his heartbeat thumped in his ears. "I'm dying anyway," he said. "Kill me if you want, but I won't help him unless you do three things." He swallowed. His throat felt like sandpaper. "First, you agree to let me and Chook go." The cool point of the knife pressed harder against his cheek.

"Second, you agree to leave our families alone forever."

Maxine bared her teeth. "You fix him!"

"Promise!" Dig's voice cracked, and he started wheezing. "You'll...leave us...alone for good...right?"

Behind her, Shiv hacked a chunk of phlegm to the floor.

Maxine's eyes screwed shut. "Yes, yes. I'll do it! Now just fix him!"

"I have...your word?"

"Yes!"

"Good. Now...for the third thing." He winced as his vision momentarily blurred. "Admit to Shiv...that we share a father."

The room fell silent. Shiv glanced up.

A sheen of sweat covered Maxine's forehead. "No," she said in a high tone. "That's not true."

"The charade's over now...just admit it."

Maxine narrowed her eyes and pushed the tip of the knife further into Dig's cheek, breaking the skin. Warm blood ran down his cheek. His pulse thumped in the side of his neck as he stared at Maxine through the slits of his swollen eyes.

"Mother," Shiv croaked, exhaling the words between laboured breaths. "You don't have to...lie anymore. I know that...he is...telling the truth."

Maxine went to speak, but the words caught in her mouth.

"You can...admit it," Shiv said. "This guy is my...half-brother."

Maxine stared out towards the deck, silent.

"Don't...let me die. Just tell me...the truth."

The room fell quiet, save for the sound of heavy breathing.

"Max," Girish stammered from the other side of the room as he tugged at the collar of his shirt. "I think it's time he knew."

Maxine closed her eyes. She was shaking, and a bead of sweat tracked down her temple.

A moment later, Dig felt the pressure from the tip of the knife ease on his cheek, and Maxine's arm lowered to her side. She turned to Shiv.

"Okay," she said. "He was your father. Does that make you feel better? He's still dead."

She glanced at Dig with a downturned mouth, then turned back to Shiv. "And you want some more truth? Your father never wanted to know about you. He pretended you didn't exist in order to preserve the image of his precious family back home in Australia. He already had a wife, and he already had a son. So when you were conceived, you were just an inconvenience." She raised her eyebrows. "Does that piece of truth make you feel good? Or maybe you would rather have not known?" Her chest rose up and down. "Maybe it would've been better to pretend that Girish was your father, than to have one that didn't want to know you are alive."

Shiv blinked and a tear dropped down his cheek.

Maxine sneered and stepped toward Dig. She lowered the knife and sliced the binding free on one hand, then cut through the other ties. "Get moving," she said. "If you can't sort him out quick smart I'm going to slice you into tiny pieces."

Dig dug into his pocket as black dots danced across his vision. His breath hitched in his chest as he fumbled the Epipen out with a shaky hand and positioned it over his thigh. The pin fired and a rush of adrenaline climbed through his body. He clenched his teeth and closed his eyes.

"What are you doing!" Maxine screamed. "Move!" She yanked his collar and pushed him to the floor. He landed in a heap beside Shiv, panting.

Shiv lay slumped against the base of the couch. His neck was a swollen pink mass. His eyebrows were drawn together. He sucked in breaths one by one and expelled them with a grimace.

Dig's body ached, but he reached into his pocket and grasped the second Epipen. He crawled forward and dragged it up to Shiv's thigh, then fired it through the skin.

"Welcome...to the family."

Over the next few minutes Dig lay beside Shiv, taking in air. The squeeze in his temples slowly released, and his lungs regained composure.

Maxine watched from the kitchen bench, leaning forward on the stone surface. Another cigarette burned in her hand. Raj and Girish remained in the corner of the room.

Eventually, the wheezing in Shiv's chest also dissipated, the colour returned to his cheeks, and his breathing slowed to a regular pace.

"Feeling better?" Maxine said. The faint trickle of the river echoed through the exterior doorway.

Shiv nodded weakly.

"Good," she said, and cleared her throat. "Because I think it's time we all put this behind us and got on with things."

Shiv stared at the ground and shook his head in the negative.

Maxine narrowed her eyes. "Got an opinion on that?"

Shiv blinked, then pursed his lips before speaking in a husky voice. "I've had enough."

Maxine butted out her cigarette, and walked across the room. "You're angry," she said. "I can understand that. But now we need to get on with business."

"Get on with business? Or get on with lying to me to settle your old scores."

"I didn't tell you for a reason. I was protecting you."

"Protecting me? You made a fool of me. You sent me over there blind, with no thought of letting me know the truth."

Dig nodded. "And you forced my dad to pass on the extracted opium. That was his side of the bargain in exchange for you keeping quiet."

Maxine turned sharply and jabbed a finger into his face. "Did you think I was going to let him just forget us?" Her face flushed red. "I didn't want to give him those hops. I didn't need the complication of dealing with distributors in Australia." She bared a set of cracked, brown teeth. "But what I *did* want was for him to be *reminded*. All the time. So I made him take the hops, but I sent Shiv over to pick up the packages every few months. So he *couldn't* forget him." Her last few words faded away, and she stared at the wall. "So he couldn't forget me."

Her attention broke, and she wiped at the corner of her eye. "He had to suffer too," she said with eyebrows drawn together. "Not just us."

The room fell into silence.

Girish turned to face the window, and Raj stood by the door with his arms folded. Shiv lay by the couch, staring at the floor, his lip quivering.

Maxine blinked and adjusted her hair. "But now it's time to move on."

"No." Shiv waved at the room. "I don't want to be part of...this...anymore." He sat forward and rubbed at his temples. "I'm out."

Maxine gave a strained smile. "Oh come on. You're just a little upset."

"Yes," Shiv said. "And the only way to stop that is to be away from you. You are...toxic."

Maxine squatted close to him, her eyes cold. "You aren't going anywhere. We are your family."

"No you're not." Shiv nodded at Girish and Raj. "Those two are your family. I'm just your bastard. Your failed history that you can't ignore. Your reminder of the guy who broke your heart—then left us both behind."

Maxine clenched her teeth. "And so your answer is to be just like him. To run away and leave me." She held up a finger. "Well you aren't going anywhere boy. You're part of this now, and you should know already that nobody walks away from this place who isn't one of us." She pointed at Dig. "Including him and his friends." Maxine nodded to the thug brothers, and they moved to stand beside her. "Do I need to add you to the list?"

"I thought you agreed to let them go?" Shiv said.

Maxine laughed. "You should know better than that."

She gestured at Jules' body in the centre of the floor. "First, we need to get rid of her." She turned to the thugs. "Drag her outside and throw her in the river." The men nodded and stepped forward.

"No!" Shiv said firmly. "Leave her."

They stopped and glanced back and forth between Shiv and Maxine.

"Do it!" Maxine shouted.

"Leave her!" Shiv repeated.

The thugs remained frozen, eyes wide.

Maxine stepped forward and slapped the bald-headed thug hard across the face. He winced and dropped his gaze to the floor. Maxine glared around the room. "Fine," she said. "I'll do it myself if I have to."

She walked to the tarpaulin and squatted over the lump that was Jules' feet, then took hold of the material and began to drag the body across the floor toward the rear door.

Shiv tried to push himself to a standing position, but his balance wavered and he dropped back to his rear—seemingly too weak to support himself.

Maxine tucked in her chin and dragged the tarpaulin further, shuffling backwards, step-by-step, moving closer to the deck—when a figure appeared behind her in the doorway to the toilet.

It was Chook, leaning against the frame, his long blonde hair matted to one side of his head. One arm was curled up against the front of his chest. The other held the metal towel rail in his grasp like a hurley stick. His jaw was set, and his eyes steely.

"He said leave her alone, you bitch." Chook lifted the rail, then swung it down, hard.

The railing bounced off the crown of Maxine's head with a ringing *clang!* and she collapsed forward to the floor, face down.

The thick-jawed thug bolted across the room. Chook stood over Maxine, panting, then lifted the metal bar and swung down a second time, smashing the pole into the back of her head with a crunch. A fine mist of blood splashed out onto the concrete like a halo, and covered Chook's arms and face.

The thug thumped into Chook, knocking him down and pinning him to the floor. The metal rail dropped to the ground with a clatter.

A deep red rivulet of blood ran from Maxine's ear and pooled across the floor.

Raj arrived beside Maxine, pulling at her shoulder, and rolled her over to her back. Her head fell to one side; her vacant eyes were heavily lidded. Blood ran from her nose and ears.

"Mother!" Raj shouted. "Can you hear me?"

Her last breath caught in her throat with a gurgle.

Raj clenched his jaw and his eyebrows knitted together.

Girish arrived beside him, holding up her limp hand. His head was tilted to one side and a tear ran down his cheek. "My darling."

Shiv remained on the couch, watching with his lips pressed together.

Raj's gaze locked on Dig and he pushed himself to his feet, his eyes wet with tears. He reached down to pick up the solid handrail from the floor. It was covered in a red sheen.

Dig tried to stand, but a wave of vertigo clouded his head and he clung to the couch for support. "Raj," he said. "Take it easy."

Raj scowled and stepped toward him, the rail dragging a groove across the concrete behind him. His lips quivered. "It's your fault."

"I didn't know."

"I don't care." He clenched his teeth and lifted the bar like a baseball bat, then planted his foot forward. Dig winced and held up a protective hand.

"No." Shiv appeared behind Raj and locked his hand around the end of the bar. Raj grimaced and tried to yank the implement away.

"No more," Shiv said.

Raj glared at him. "You aren't in charge of me."

"I am now," Shiv said firmly. He stepped forward and stood over him. "I'm taking over things now. Got that?"

Raj looked from Shiv to Girish, and wrinkled his nose. "Taking over? Who gives you the right?" Tears ran down his face as he tried to wrestle the bar away from Shiv's grasp. "You're nothing but a bastard. A treacherous *bastard*."

Shiv shoved Raj in the chest, and Raj landed heavily on his rear beside his father. Girish placed an arm around his shoulders, and he hitched in sobs.

Shiv's chest rose up and down. "Anyone else here got an issue with that?" He eyed the thugs. They shook their heads.

Shiv turned to face Dig with the bar still hanging from his grasp. Dig pursed his lips and met his gaze. Silence hung in the air for a long moment. A rivulet of blood tracked down the bar and dropped onto the floor.

"You need to go now," Shiv said.

Dig wiped his forehead with the back of a shaking hand, and nodded. "I'm taking Chook and Jules with me."

Shiv paused. "Okay. But you say nothing about this place. You say she was attacked by a swarm somewhere back in the hills."

"Fine. And we go home, and you leave us be. Forever."

"But you get no hops from us. The business is over for you, and you tell no one about our production."

Dig took a deep breath. "Okay."

Girish watched from the floor with narrow eyes. "No Shiv, Max wouldn't let that happen."

"We aren't doing things Max's way anymore." Shiv tapped the bar against the stone kitchen bench and glared at Dig. "Seriously. Not a word. Or I personally come back for you, your family, and Chook's family, one by one."

"You've nothing to worry about."

Shiv stared at him for a moment, then nodded. "Okay. Take our truck to town, but leave it at the tracks."

The thick-jawed thug removed his knee from Chook's back. Chook crawled across the floor to his sister's body. He leaned in to see her swollen and battered face, and his face contorted in a grimace.

Dig turned to Chook. "You hear that?" Chook raised an eyebrow and nodded, then wrapped the tarpaulin carefully around Jules like a blanket. He lifted her over his shoulder, straightened, and shuffled out of the building toward the truck.

Dig rubbed at the back of his neck, then turned to the men in the room and nodded. He took two steps toward the door, then stopped and turned back. He glanced around the room and pursed his lips. "I'm...sorry," he said. "For everything." He gave a small shrug. "For...Dad I mean."

Shiv's eyes dropped to the floor before he looked up again. "Was he...a good guy?" he said. "You know...as a dad."

Dig gave a weak smile. "Yeah. He was."

Shiv's forehead creased.

Dig watched him for a moment. "You already knew about Dad, right? Before today."

Shiv folded his arms. "Why would you say that?"

"Back at our house in Sydney, when you broke in. You smashed our family picture in the dryer. That always seemed weird, but I think I understand why now."

Shiv's eyes flared and he glanced back at Raj and Girish. A flush crept across his cheeks. "I had guessed," he said. "But I still wanted to hear her say it."

Dig nodded slowly. "Look, if you ever want to come and visit, and see some photos or something—"

"No," Shiv said. "No thanks."

"Okay."

The half-brothers stood in an awkward silence. From the carpark, a car door thudded shut. The wind whispered through the overhanging roots of the banyan trees beside the deck. Raj and Girish kneeled together on the floor of the room, and watched Dig with narrowed eyes.

"I'm sorry it ended up this way guys," Dig said, and hoisted his pack over his shoulder.

There was no answer. He turned for the door.

He stepped out into the sunlight. Chook sat in the passenger seat of the hi-rail truck with his eyes closed. The tarpaulin was wedged on the back tray, up against the cab. Dig eased into the driver's seat.

He adjusted the rear view mirror and caught sight of himself. Dirt was caked through his greasy hair. A red triangle was sliced out of his cheek, matted with dried blood.

But he didn't care. He was going home.

He fired the machine into life and pushed it into gear. They rumbled out of the carpark and followed the dirt road that led up to the railway tracks. As they reached the rails, Dig eased the machine to a stop. "Know how to work the track wheels on this thing?"

Chook shook his head.

Dig prodded at the switches on the dash. The wipers squealed across a dry windscreen, before a whir emanated from below as the rail wheels dropped and slotted into position. The truck lurched forward on the tracks.

As they moved up the rise, Dig glanced at the field of hops spread out below them, and sighed.

The tunnel opening neared, and Dig dropped the truck out of gear and eased it to a stop outside the entrance.

Chook opened his eyes. "What?"

"Just give me a sec. I'll be back." Dig stepped out of the truck. Chook frowned.

A few minutes later Dig returned, and they were on their way again.

As the truck entered the tunnel, they wound the windows tightly shut. He was in no mood to deal with hornets inside the cab.

But his fears were unfounded. As the truck passed through the heart of the tunnel the headlights illuminated the smoking frame of the cabinet. Dig brought the machine to a stop and leaned forward over the dash.

On the ballast floor lay the hulking skeleton of the nest—black, smouldering, and split in two. Scattered around it were piles of blackened hornet carcasses, twisted and fried. Dig nodded to himself.

To one side of the nest, against the tunnel wall, Dig's eyes caught on a second crumpled lump of fabric. He squinted at it, then sat back in his seat. He turned to Chook, but his eyes were closed.

Dig took hold of the door handle. He stepped out to the ground and skirted through the headlight beams at the front of the truck, then lifted the lump of fabric.

It was Jules' backpack. As he returned to the cab he slammed the door behind him.

He threw the bag into Chook's lap. Chook opened his eyes, startled.

"That was Jules' bag," Dig said.

Chook looked down at his lap.

"I think there's a chunk of cash in there. Something like sixty thousand. It's yours now."

Chook raised an eyebrow.

Dig crunched the truck into gear again, heading toward Hampi.

Sometime later, they stopped at a building entrance of white concrete columns and faded glass.

"Hospital," Dig said.

Chook blinked and stretched. "Okay."

"You want some help?"

"No," he said. "I've got her."

"Going to get your hand sorted?"

"Yep."

Dig bit at his lip. "Look—"

"Don't worry," Chook interrupted. "I won't say anything. Just like your arsehole brother wanted."

Dig nodded, and they turned and gave each other a stiff embrace. Chook stepped out of the car, lifted his sister out of the back tray, and carried her into the front entrance of the hospital.

Dig watched them go, then drove back into the street.

A few minutes later he parked the truck beside the old railway line. He wedged the keys above the sun visor and stepped out onto the dirt.

He hiked back to the main street of Hampi bazaar. It was early afternoon and crowded. Heat rose from the dirt and clouded his vision to the end of the street. Dust tickled his nose.

As he reached the bus terminal he stopped, checked the timetable, and continued past it until he stood outside the shopfront of *Helpful Hari's Tourist Information*. He pushed through the door.

Hari's face was unshaven and his hair tousled. He raised his eyebrows as Dig entered, and Dig frowned.

"You lost another one?" Hari said. "The motorbike?"

Dig nodded.

Hari shook his head. "Well this one's going to cost you. Two thousand American."

Dig extracted his wallet and sifted through it. There were only a few dirty rupee notes remaining. "What if I don't have that much?"

"Then I call my friends at the police station."

"No. We don't need to do that." He scratched at his face, then after a moment he pulled his backpack to his chest and searched inside. He glanced through the front window, then leaned in close to Hari, whispering. "Look. I know you deal in some pretty unorthodox stuff, right?"

Hari also leaned in close. "It depends."

"Would you take some drugs as payment?"

Hari blinked, then turned to his nephew. "Troy!" he shouted. "Cameras!"

The computer screen blinked off, then lit up a bank of grainy CCTV images. Dig recognised the front door of the shop amongst them. The boy studied the feed for a moment, then nodded to Hari.

Hari straightened his tie and turned to Dig. "What have you got?"

Dig took a second glance at the front window, then reached into his bag. Down at the base, still nestled in the hidden compartment, was the brown brick that Jules had concealed inside. Dig tugged at it until it pulled free, and handed it to Hari.

Hari stiffened, then dropped the brick to the desk behind the counter. He leant down and gave a long sniff, then looked back up at Dig with wide eyes and wobbled his head. "Yes," he said. "This can work. Where did you get it from?"

"I can't say."

"Is this all you have?"

"I think so," Dig said. "Let me check." He reached into the bag again, pushing below the false bottom. His fingers came upon a second package, and he pulled it out. It was white, and had the consistency of powder.

Hari's mouth dropped open and he grabbed it quickly to conceal it behind the counter. A rustling of packaging could be heard, and then another long sniff. Moments later, Hari's head shot back up. His pupils were large and his shoulders stiff. He fumbled with his shirt cuffs. "Er, I could be interested in this too," he said. "How much do you want?"

Dig shrugged. "How much you offering?"

"For the two packages? Hmmm, say...three hundred thousand American?"

Dig stared at Hari. "Are you kidding?"

Hari frowned. "Okay!" he said. "You can also waive the lost motorbike...but that's my final offer." He tilted his head. "Deal?"

Dig blinked rapidly. "Sure."

"Good, good. Now just let me get rid of this." He shouted across the room. "Troy! Watch the desk." The boy pushed to his feet and walked over to stand beside Dig. He produced a small handgun from his back pocket and held it loosely at his waist, watching Dig from the corner of his eye, blank-faced.

Hari slunk out to the back room. There was a fiddling of keys, and a loud creak. He returned moments later with a wad of notes, and held it out low at the side of the counter. "Three hundred K," Hari whispered. "I promise."

Dig took the wad of notes and pushed it into his bag, deep into the bottom compartment. Butterflies danced in his stomach. "Okay then."

"Good to do business with you." They both stood stiffly with their hands in their pockets.

"Well, I'll be going then."

"Will you be back with more?"

"No," Dig said. "I don't plan to ever come back to Hampi. But no offence or anything. It's a nice town and all that."

Hari wobbled his head and cocked his eyebrows. "You need a bus ticket?"

"Yes," Dig said, smiling. "I'll take a bus ticket."

19

A COUPLE OF DAYS LATER, Dig's taxi pulled up outside the family home back in Sydney. He paid the driver, stepped out of the car, and watched the brewery while the taxi reversed out of the driveway.

He walked down the drive and entered through the side door. Jake drove the forklift through the building, transporting a pallet of beer to the delivery truck. He wore blue overalls, and the shelves around him were all but bare. The forklift drifted to a stop. He stepped out, smiling, and embraced Dig with his good arm. "You made it."

Dig nodded. "How's the hand?"

Jake shrugged and held up the bandage. "Getting better."

"Got things under control?"

"Yeah I think so." He pointed at the shelves around him. "Apart from the fact that we're nearly out of stock. How'd things finish up?"

"It was mental."

"Dig!" said his mother, standing in the door. "I saw your taxi pull up." She gave him a solid hug. "How was your business meeting?"

Dig's forehead creased and he shoved a hand into his pocket. "To be honest," he said. "It didn't go that well. Our supplier can't supply us with hops anymore, meaning we can't produce Buckley's Chance."

Dig's mother put her hand to her mouth. Jake dropped his head and cursed under his breath. "So that's it then," he said. "We just lost the house." He turned away and laced his hands in his hair.

Dig's mother looked from Jake to Dig with wide eyes. "Is that true?"

Dig paused. "Not necessarily."

Jake frowned. "And how do you figure that?"

"The supplier offered us some compensation for our losses."

"Huh?"

Dig reached into his backpack, dug around at the base, then threw the wad of notes to his brother. "Three hundred thousand. In cash."

Jake examined the money. "How the hell did you manage that?"

"I'll tell you later. But, by my calcs, that gives us a couple of years where we can keep the mortgage paid off, and in the meantime we can work on getting the production of Buckley's Chance going again."

Jake raised his eyebrows. "Sure," he said. "But aren't you missing one important fact here? We still don't have the hops."

Dig smiled. "I think we can do it." He reached deep into his pack again, down inside the hidden compartment, and held up some wiry brown roots.

"Just before I left the brewery," he said. "I took the liberty of grabbing a handful of rhizomes."

"What's a rhizome?" said his mother.

"The roots of the hop vine. They're still alive, and ready to be planted."

Jake smiled. "You cheeky bastard!"

Dig's mother frowned. "But, can a few vines produce enough hops?"

"Not straight away," Dig said. "But I've been studying up on cutting and transplanting, and by the time we're a couple of years down the track, we should have a reasonable crop developed—enough to get a few solid batches going."

"And no reliance on suppliers," Jake said, smiling broadly.

"Exactly."

"Well that's good...isn't it?" said Dig's mum.

"Very good," Jake said, and put an arm around Dig's shoulder, shaking him side-to-side. "Well played bro, well played."

Dig's mother planted a kiss on his cheek. "I'm going to make some hamburgers to celebrate," she said, and turned back to the house. As she passed through the doorway, she stopped and turned back around. "And you know you two, I just want to say that it's good to see you actually getting on. Can we try to keep that going?"

They shrugged.

His mother smiled and left the room.

Jake turned to Dig. "Was that bullshit?"

"Nope," Dig said. "All true—except the part about compensation." He followed his mother out the door.

Jake followed close behind. "So where'd you get the cash from?"

Dig stopped at the patch of grass beside the house, and looked up at the roof. The sky was clear and blue and the sun was warm. "It's a long story," he said. "How about we grab some beanbags and beers and sit up on the roof? It's an awesome view up there, and I'll tell you everything."

"Now you're starting to sound like Dad." Jake shook his head and sighed. "The ladder's down the side. I'll get the beers."

Dig watched him go, then crouched to claw at the dirt near the base of the chimney until he had an elbow deep hole. He retrieved the rhizomes and placed them vertically in the hole before filling it back up with dirt.

"Already starting your crop?" Jake held out a bottle of *Buckley's Chance*.

"No point waiting," Dig took the beer. "Just needs a bit of moisture." He poured a third of it into the ground around the rhizome.

Jake poured out some of his own bottle. "Start of a new era."

Dig glanced up to the roof of the house. Against the blue sky, the shape of a small bird floated down from the trees and landed on the top of the chimney. Its feathers were green and blue, and its neck a pale yellow. It lifted its head and chirped out a melodic tune.

Dig smiled. It was good to be home.

ENJOYED THE BOOK?

Please consider leaving an honest review at the place you bought it, or at sites such as amazon.com or goodreads.com, or liking it on Facebook.

ACKNOWLEDGMENTS

This story is for my father, PK, who passed away suddenly during its writing. I wish he could have read it. Huge thanks also go to my wife, Angela, who supported me throughout the writing process.

I'm grateful that two people who didn't know me agreed to be beta readers—and ended up acting more like structural editors. The time, effort and brutal honesty they dished out helped me more than I could imagine. Jason Noble and Alice Miller are both great writers, look out for their work.

Thanks also go to the copy editor, Sophie Dougall; the cover artist, Derek Murphy; Owie for his modeling work on the front cover; and my friends who helped me choose the title and cover design.

And finally thanks to you, the reader, for taking the time to read it. Maybe we can meet here again one day.

MJK

ABOUT THE AUTHOR

M. J. Kelly lives in Sydney, Australia with his wife and three children.

News on his future books can be found at **mjkellybooks.com**

FRIENDS OF

THE AMBER TRAIL

www.ingramcontent.com/pod-product-compliance
Lightning Source LLC
Chambersburg PA
CBHW050029180626
46810CB00002B/636